"I won't do it. I won't sign the divorce petition."

"No problem. I'll sign it. As long as one of us has been resident here. And we qualify on just about all grounds." Jack's eyes narrowed. "Except impotence."

"I'll contest the divorce," Callie said.

"You can't contest irreconcilable differences."

"Yes, I can—and that's not all I can do. The judge can order us to attend counseling for a month."

He waved a hand dismissively. "I'm not doing any counseling."

"You never know. You might even benefit from some relationship counseling."

"We don't have a relationship," he snarled, losing all pretense at calm.

Dear Reader,

One thing you can count on these days is that things change. All the time, whether we want them to or not.

In *The Groom Came Back*, Dr. Jack Mitchell's original purpose in marrying Callie Summers years ago was good, maybe even noble—he rescued her from a custody battle and made sure she could stay living with his parents, who cherished her company. But over time, his reasons for staying married changed: Callie's presence meant he could stop thinking about his family, and not feel guilty about staying away.

Eight years later, when it's finally convenient for Jack to go home and get a divorce, he discovers something else has changed. His shy, awkward bride has grown into a gorgeous woman who's not going to let him leave town—and his family—without a fight.

The battle between the high-flying neurosurgeon and the home-loving florist is on....

I hope you enjoy this story—please e-mail me at abby@abbygaines.com and let me know what you think.

To read a couple of extra, After the End scenes for *The Groom Came Back*, visit the For Readers page at www.abbygaines.com.

Sincerely,

Abby Gaines

THE GROOM CAME BACK
Abby Gaines

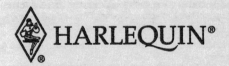

TORONTO • NEW YORK • LONDON
AMSTERDAM • PARIS • SYDNEY • HAMBURG
STOCKHOLM • ATHENS • TOKYO • MILAN • MADRID
PRAGUE • WARSAW • BUDAPEST • AUCKLAND

Recycling programs
for this product may
not exist in your area.

ISBN-13: 978-0-373-71539-8
ISBN-10:   0-373-71539-0

THE GROOM CAME BACK

Copyright © 2009 by Abby Gaines.

www.eHarlequin.com

Printed in U.S.A.

ABOUT THE AUTHOR

Abby Gaines wrote her first romance novel as a teenager. She typed it up and sent it to Mills & Boon in London, who promptly rejected it. A flirtation with a science fiction novel never really got off the ground, so Abby put aside her writing ambitions as she went to college, then began her working life at IBM. When she and her husband had their first baby, Abby worked from home as a freelance business journalist...and soon after that the urge to write romance resurfaced. It was another five long years before Abby sold her first novel to Harlequin Superromance in 2006. She now writes for Harlequin NASCAR as well as Harlequin Superromance.

Abby lives with her husband and children—and a labradoodle and a kitten—in a house with enough stairs to keep her fit and a sun-filled office whose sea view provides inspiration for the funny, tender romances she loves to write. Visit her at www.abbygaines.com.

Books by Abby Gaines

HARLEQUIN SUPERROMANCE
1397—WHOSE LIE IS IT ANYWAY?
1414—MARRIED BY MISTAKE
1480—THE DIAPER DIARIES

HARLEQUIN NASCAR
BACK ON TRACK
FULLY ENGAGED

For Victoria Curran, with thanks for your support—
and your patience!
Thanks for helping me become a better writer.

CHAPTER ONE

CALLIE SUMMERS RECOGNIZED her husband the moment he walked in the door of Fresher Flowers. He, however, clearly had no idea who she was.

Her smile of welcome faded in the face of Jack Mitchell's utter lack of recognition. Could eight years, ten thousand dollars' worth of orthodontic treatments and a great haircut make that much difference?

Jack ducked a hanging basket of trailing clematis and stepped around the center display of post-Arbor Day markdowns. As he neared Callie, his glance skimmed her sky-blue tank—she'd grown breasts since she'd last seen him, too—and swooped down her short blue-and-white skirt to her ankles, then back up to her face. There was nothing as blatant as admiration in his gray-green eyes—more a keen observation.

You didn't get to be a top neurosurgeon without developing powers of observation, Callie supposed. Even if his *memory* was somewhat deficient.

"Hi," he said. "I hear you're the best florist in Parkvale." Had his smile been that sexy eight years ago?

Of course not. At seventeen, she'd viewed Jack's

twenty-six years as a source of comfort, of protection. Besides, those hadn't been happy days.

"Good morn—uh—afternoon." Callie's attempt at formality to mark this one-sided reunion fizzled as she struggled to remember if it was past twelve yet; she closed at twelve-thirty on Saturdays. She finished arranging stems of gerbera—orange and crimson and pink—in a galvanized steel bucket set on an iron stand. Then she stepped forward, brushing her hands against her skirt, in case Jack had actually recognized her and planned to shake her hand or…something. "I like to think I do a great job for my clients—not that Alice at Darling Buds isn't very talented," she added hastily.

She totally lacked the killer instinct she needed for Fresher Flowers to flourish on the scale her loan officer demanded.

Jack's smile turned confiding. "I'm in a hurry. I need—" he glanced around in the blankly searching manner common to most men who walked into Callie's store "—some flowers."

She might be short on killer instinct, but her sense of mischief was in full working order. "Are they for your wife?"

He recoiled. "I'm not—"

She saw in his frown the sudden uncomfortable realization that here in Parkvale, Tennessee, he was indeed married. Even if no one else knew about it.

He folded his arms and looked down at her— she'd forgotten how tall he was—his mouth a wry twist. "They're for my mother, Brenda Mitchell. Do you know her?"

"I know her well. She's wonderful." Callie let a trace of what she felt for Brenda into her voice. But although Jack picked up on it—his dark eyebrows lifted a fraction—there was still no flash of recognition. Nor did he endorse her comment about his mother.

So much for Brenda's insistence that Jack missed his family. That he *wanted* to come home from his prestigious job at Oxford University Hospital in England. That he *would* have come home sooner, if only there wasn't always another life to save.

Callie had suspected for a long time that Jack had simply outgrown his family. Only she knew that, if he had his way, this visit would sever one of the last of his ties.

She held his gaze and smiled warmly, giving him one more chance to click. "How much would you like to spend on your mom?"

"Since you know her, how about you make up something she'd like, without worrying about the price?" He glanced at his watch—platinum not steel, she guessed—then out the window, checking on the black Jaguar parked in the street.

"How generous of you." A little nip, not strong enough to qualify as a bite.

Now those expressive eyebrows drew together. "Excuse me?"

You can't make up for eight years of absence with a hundred-dollar bunch of flowers. "Brenda likes irises," she said, with a fierceness that was at first on Brenda's behalf, because she wouldn't dream of criticizing her darling son, and then for Callie herself. "And delphiniums."

He blinked. "Irises and delphiniums it is, then," he said in a calm tone she could imagine him using with a patient while he waited for the men in white coats.

If she'd told him Brenda liked carnations and pansies he wouldn't have known any better.

The answer to the question that had plagued Callie for weeks—*how will I feel when I see Jack?*—hit her with the force of a hurricane.

She was furious.

BY THE TIME Jack climbed back into the Jaguar, the best rental car available from the airport in Memphis, nearly all the stores on Bicentennial Square had closed. This place was dead on the weekends, and only marginally breathing during the week. He glanced at his watch as he pulled out into the light Saturday traffic, and wondered what time it was in Oxford and whether he could call this afternoon to check up on his patients. Wondered what time the Marquette County courthouse opened on Monday.

How soon he could get a divorce.

Maybe he should, as the cute but moody florist had suggested, have bought flowers for *her.* His wife. Callista Jane Summers, according to the youthful scrawl on the marriage license application. But a bunch of yellow roses wouldn't suffice to thank her.

He stopped at one of Parkvale's dozen sets of traffic lights, then headed out of the square on tree-lined Main Street.

The elms, planted the year Jack was born, had grown taller in his absence. Yet the town itself had shrunk. It had always been too small, and now was Lilliputian. He'd no sooner started down Main when it was time to hang a left on Forsyth, and only seconds later, he was turning right into Stables Lane.

The narrow, dead-end avenue wasn't much longer than a stone's throw. A couple of cars were parked with two wheels on the sidewalk to allow passage. Jack pulled into his parents' driveway, behind his father's Ford Ranger pickup.

He left everything in the car except the flowers, wrapped in layers of lilac and green paper. The florist had told him what they were, but apart from the irises he'd forgotten. She'd done a nice job, that girl in the sexy blue tank. Jack had been surprised to learn from the guy at the gas station that Parkvale now boasted four florists. Eight years ago, he'd bought a corsage for his…bride…at the town's sole flower shop, conveniently situated across the road from the hospital.

He gripped the flowers tighter, and steeled himself as he headed up the walk. For the overdue reunion with his parents. For the inevitable encounter with Callista Jane Summers.

Dealing with Callie would be the easy part, he reminded himself. She was a good kid, and fully aware of the favor he'd done her. And although her e-mails had come irritatingly close to nagging about the need for him to come home, she wanted the same thing as he did where their marriage was concerned.

Whereas his parents… It had been easier to stay away than get their hopes up about him coming back and "settling down."

What was the bet that within half an hour he'd be

fending off suggestions that he switch from neurosurgery to dermatology or geriatrics or something equally unlikely, and apply for a job in Parkvale?

His mother must have heard the car, because she showed up in the doorway, hopping from one foot to another like a kid of ten. "Jack!" Her delighted squeal gave him an unexpected lift. He took the porch steps in two strides, and grabbed her for a hug.

"You're so tall, I can't believe it." Brenda squeezed him with the strength of a woman who'd had years of kneading her own bread dough.

"Cut it out, Mom. I'm no taller than I was when we caught up in New York last year."

"I forgot then, too," she said, unashamed.

"Maybe you're getting shorter." That earned him a swat on the back as he stepped over the threshold. He turned to hand her the flowers, which hadn't suffered from being squashed in that hug.

"Jack, they're gorgeous." Brenda sniffed deeply at the bouquet, then sent him a sly smile. "I'll bet I know where you got these."

"The best florist in town," he said easily.

His mom beamed. "Isn't she just?"

Something about that beam, which smacked of personal pride, rang alarm bells in Jack's head.

Then his mom said, "Everyone's here to see you, sweetie. I put on a light lunch," and he forgot about the florist.

"Everyone" meant a bunch of Mitchell relatives, and a "light lunch" meant a groaning buffet table, doubtless including his mother's signature dish, Parkvale Curried Chicken Salad. He'd kind of missed

Parkvale Curried Chicken Salad, which bore no resemblance to anything from India and had only a passing acquaintance with curry powder.

Brenda shepherded him into the living room of the Victorian house. High-ceilinged, deep-windowed, it at least was still the size he remembered. "He's here," she announced.

Uncle Frank and Aunt Nancy occupied the window seat. Their daughter, Sarah, held hands on the couch with a dark-haired man, and Jack vaguely recalled news of an engagement, plans for a June wedding. The two guys over by the bookcase must be Mark and Jason, Sarah's older brothers. They'd both bulked up in eight years and Mark—or was it Jason?—had a serious facial hair thing going.

"Son, it's great to see you." Jack's father caught him in an easy hug. He must have closed the hardware store early, since Dan usually liked to put in a full day on Saturday. "I mean in the flesh," Dan joked, "not just on TV."

"Good to see you, too, Dad." Jack shook his hand.

Dan put a possessive arm around Brenda, who leaned into him with the loving look that Jack forever associated with his parents.

Situation normal. It didn't take a medical degree to see everything was as it had always been. Whatever point Callie had been trying to make in her e-mails, she was wrong.

Jack moved around the room, greeting his relatives, being introduced to the fiancé, accepting congratulations for the TV documentary that had recently aired on his pioneering surgical techniques. He'd completed his circuit, said his fourth "No, I'm not back for good" and accepted a beer, when through the picture window, he saw a white Honda coupe pull up across the end of his parents' driveway, blocking his car in.

Jack tugged at the collar of his shirt. He reminded himself he could leave town anytime he liked; it was crazy to feel as if his escape route had been cut off.

A woman got out of the car. Huh, the florist. Jack patted his back pocket. Nope, he hadn't left his wallet in the store.

She walked up the path, her stride purposeful, her hips swinging. From this distance, he got perspective on her figure, which really was great.

"Uh, Mom..." He gestured toward the window.

"There she is," Brenda said, pleased.

The florist hadn't been kidding when she said she knew his mom well. So well that she walked in the front door without knocking or waiting to be admitted. Everyone in the room greeted her with familiarity, a ragged succession of heys and hellos.

"Sweetie, you did a wonderful job with these flowers." It took Jack a second to realize that his mom was talking to the woman, not him. Her use of the family endearment "sweetie" niggled, no matter that in his younger years he'd derided it.

"I was looking at some old photos the other day," Brenda said to Jack, "and I couldn't believe how Callie has changed. I'm amazed you recognized her."

Who would have guessed Jack had a degree from Harvard Medical School and postgraduate qualifications from Oxford University, when it took him five long seconds to realize what should have been glaringly obvious the moment he'd stepped into that damn shop?

The woman standing six feet away from him, lips curved in a smile but blue eyes sparking with an emotion that was far from friendly, was Callie. Callista Jane Summers. The woman he'd married.

"Actually, Brenda, he didn't recognize me," she said. "And I'm afraid I was naughty. I didn't tell him."

Jack knew from that flash in her eyes there'd been more than mischief behind her omission. What the heck was going on?

Brenda laughed, delighted. "That's just gorgeous. Jack, did you really have no idea?"

Without taking his eyes off Callie, he said to his mom, "You never told me she's a florist. I thought she renovates houses."

"I buy houses and do them up in my spare time so I can sell them again." Callie met his gaze full on. She didn't need to tell him that, dammit; she'd been using his money to fund her little DIY venture. "But I trained as a florist, and I've had my own store nearly a year."

"Now that you know who she is—" Brenda patted his arm "—you can greet her properly."

His head snapped around. Out of the corner of his eye, he saw Callie's do the same. Surely Mom didn't mean...

"Give her a kiss," Brenda urged, just as she used to make him kiss his sister, Lucy, on her birthday.

He looked at Callie, saw in her eyes the acknowledgment that any refusal would cause more trouble than either of them needed. He moved toward her, just as she took a halting step in his direction.

She offered him her right cheek. He brushed it with his lips, and though the contact lasted only a fraction of a second, it was long enough to feel the contrast between the satiny smoothness of her skin and the dry hardness of his lips. Long enough to pick up the scent of jasmine and roses and something else uniquely floral. *She's a florist, so of course she smells like a garden.*

She pulled away fast, leaving Jack feeling as if his lips were stranded on a street corner. Brenda murmured her approval.

Callie clasped her hands behind her back so she wouldn't rub her cheek where Jack had kissed it. Her brain faltered and she found herself saying, "So, how long are you in town?"

She knew, of course. She was the one who'd told him he needed to be resident in the county for thirty days before they could file for a no-fault divorce. The quizzical furrow in his brow confirmed that not only did he distrust her thanks to her "joke," he now doubted her mental capacity.

"He's here for a month," Brenda said happily. "Such a treat for us that he was able to convince the hospital to let him go that long."

"Lucky us," Callie said.

"I can't wait to reintroduce him around town," his mother said. "I'm thinking a walk in the park on Monday, the school board meeting on Tuesday—"

"Just leave him some time to come by the store," Dan interrupted.

"I hope to also get up to Memphis to visit the neurological team at Northcross Hospital," Jack said. He glanced at his watch, as if counting the hours and minutes until he could board a 747 and raise a champagne glass in a toast to his escape.

You're not going anywhere, Callie told him silently. "If you're looking for a medical fix, you can always check out the new geriatric ward at Parkvale Hospital," she said. "They say it's state-of-the-art for a facility of its size."

Brenda had asked Callie to make the suggestion. "You do it, sweetie. I wouldn't want him to think I'm pressuring him to move back here," she'd said, as she polished the silverware for today's lunch for the third time.

Jack's shoulders were rigid, but his expression neutral, as he said, "I'm a pediatric neurosurgeon, specializing in vascular malformations of the brain. I have no interest in geriatrics." He'd reverted to that calm tone he'd used in her shop. He definitely thought Callie wasn't the sharpest thorn on the rose.

"You mean, other than your parents." Callie grinned at Brenda to show she didn't seriously consider the woman a geriatric. Then she directed a squinty-eyed glare at Jack, a warning that she wasn't about to tolerate his lack of interest in his family.

"If you have something in your eye, I could take a look," he said helpfully.

Any thought that he'd misunderstood vanished when Callie read the return message in his hard gaze: *my relationship with my parents is none of your business.*

You made it my business, Dr. Selfish. There was one good thing about the way he was living down to her expectations; she no longer felt bad about that little lie she'd told him. She composed her features, declined his offer of medical assistance and removed the kid gloves. "If you want to know what's been happening the past eight years, I'll be happy to fill you in."

Surprise flickered across his face, as if he wasn't used to people disobeying even his unspoken orders.

"Thanks, but Mom sends me regular updates. You're still living with my folks?"

Only Callie heard the slight emphasis on the *my*. Only she recognized his question for what it was: a reminder that she'd benefited from their marriage, too. It had extricated her from an unpleasant custody battle and allowed her to continue living with Brenda and Dan.

"Not at the moment." Callie grabbed a flower-shaped bowl of peanuts from the sideboard. If she didn't have something to do with her hands, she might slug Jack. "I move in and out, depending on the stage of my latest renovation project." She offered the nuts around.

"My rule is that if the house she's working on doesn't have a functioning kitchen and bathroom, she has to live here." Dan helped himself to the peanuts, then settled into his recliner.

"Why don't you kids sit down so you can have a good chat?" Brenda tried to usher Callie and Jack toward the two-seater couch. Jack didn't move. Neither did Callie. She had the crazy thought that whoever sat first would lose this battle. Unwilling to ignore Brenda, she leaned against the sideboard.

"Handy for you," Jack commented, "having this place to come back to when you need it."

She bristled. Was he forgetting their secret wedding had freed him to go back to his illustrious career?

She hadn't seen it that way at the time, and she liked to think he hadn't, either. She'd barely known Jack. He'd been working in Boston even before she moved in with the Mitchells—but she'd figured him for a decent guy whose instinct was to protect his parents from further hurt. With her mother's encouragement, Callie had accepted that protection for herself, too.

She hadn't had a choice.

"We love having Callie around," Brenda said. "The house seems so empty when she's not here—" she waved a hand at the packed-to-the-gills living room "—but at least we know she'll always come back."

Callie knew any reference to Jack's prolonged absence was unintentional. But his mouth tightened.

"Quite a lovefest you have going with my parents," he murmured.

Whose fault was that? she wanted to ask. Somewhere along the line, their marriage had become a means for Jack to abdicate his family responsibilities to her.

"Callie is family," Dan said, almost sharply. "She's been a daughter to us ever since…"

No one needed him to complete the sentence. *Ever since Lucy died.*

Callie saw the flicker of pain on Brenda's features. Darn it, Callie still missed Lucy, too, especially at this time of year. Jack needed to confront the reality of being his parents' only surviving child. Before his month here was up, she wanted his commitment to helping his mom and to being an active part of his parents' lives as they aged. He didn't have to live in Parkvale—that might bore him into an early grave and defeat the purpose—but she did expect him to act like a son. To improve his current performance a zillion percent.

"Much as I love you guys—" she kept her tone light, not wanting thoughts of Lucy to dampen Brenda's joy in the day "—Jack's your family more than I'll ever be." She beamed at the prodigal son, raised her voice and threw down the gauntlet. "Welcome home, Jack. May this be the first of many visits."

Aunt Nancy clapped in agreement, and a couple of the cousins cheered. Brenda hugged her son.

"Thanks, Callie," he said, his jaw tight, as if he'd bitten into a bad apple but was too polite to spit it out.

Callie saw in his eyes the intention to perform a medical misadventure on her if she didn't drop the subject. She straightened her spine, forced her smile wider, sunnier. Standing this close, he looked taller than he had at the shop. Broader than he had eight years ago. And less friendly. Jack Mitchell was no doting but forgetful son in need of a gentle nudge. He was too self-centered, too famous, and he'd grown too big for his small-town roots.

Brenda moved to the doorway, called for attention. "Time for lunch, folks."

Just as Jack suspected, in the dining room, the 1970s rosewood-veneered table was laden with so much food, he could scarcely see Brenda's best lace tablecloth. His ever-considerate relatives each stood back and waited for the others to serve themselves potato salad, assorted roast vegetables, thick slices of beef sirloin and dollops of Parkvale Curried Chicken Salad.

If Jack hadn't started the ball rolling, they'd have still been there at four o'clock, saying "You first" and "No, after you."

The dining table only sat six people, so they dispersed back to the living room to eat. Between mouthfuls of superbly tender beef—he did miss his mom's cooking—Jack chatted with his parents, all the time aware of Callie talking to Uncle Frank over by the window. She laughed at something Frank said, and the sound was musical, with none of the faux friendliness she'd used on Jack.

Sensing his scrutiny, she looked across at him.

He had two abiding memories of their wedding. One was the dumb joke she'd made—out of nerves, he knew, so he'd struggled to hide his irritation. The other was of Callie's glance sliding away from his. The floor, her bitten fingernails, the air above his head, *everything* had been easier to look at than Jack.

Now, he felt as if she'd been examining him since the moment he walked into her shop. Her eyes were the brilliant blue found in some Renaissance paintings he'd admired at the Louvre. And like the Mona Lisa's, they seemed to follow him everywhere. Unlike the Mona Lisa, there was nothing mysterious about Callie's expression. Jack knew anger when he saw it.

The room suddenly felt stifling, although outside it was only in the mid-seventies.

He glanced away. Callie was like a kid sister. Which meant he wasn't about to go noticing her eyes or her figure or anything else about her. She probably thought it was her job in life to bug him.

Unfortunately for her, getting riled wasn't on his agenda. He was here to see his parents and to end his marriage. Simple.

He set his plate down on the sideboard. "Mom, I'll get my bag out of the car. Am I in my old room?"

His mother's brow creased. "I guess…if you don't mind the color."

It had always been navy blue.

"I moved into your room five years ago," Callie explained, breaking off her chat with Frank. She was obviously listening in to Jack's conversations, as well as watching his every move. "I painted it lilac and stenciled a floral border in carmine and magenta."

What the hell colors were carmine and magenta? Ones Jack wouldn't like, going by her smirk.

Jack's sense of grievance swelled. First there'd been her failure to tell him who she was, then her subtle sniping. And now, her unmistakable pleasure in forcing him to sleep in a room whose color scheme would have him talking an octave higher by morning.

Jack wondered if any of Parkvale's lawyers worked weekends.

CHAPTER TWO

"BEND FORWARD, dear." Aunt Nancy's voice was muffled by a mouthful of pins.

Obediently, Callie leaned over. The scooped bodice of the champagne-colored bridesmaid's dress gaped open.

"Goodness," Nancy said, "that's just about indecent."

"Pretty, though," Brenda said.

When Callie would have straightened, Nancy tapped her on the arm. "Let me pin it first, dear."

"Mom, if you think Callie's dress is indecent, wait till you see mine," the bride called from the dressing room attached to Nancy's basement sewing studio. Nancy was semiretired from her dressmaking business, but the studio had seen a lot of action since Sarah announced her engagement.

"I had a neckline up to here when I got married." Nancy touched her chin, ignoring the fact that her daughter couldn't see. "I don't understand why you girls want to flaunt it all in church."

She finished pinning the seam on one side of the dress, so Callie was now flaunting lopsided. Nancy moved around to her left.

The door to the studio opened. "Sweetie," Brenda said, "I haven't seen the bride yet. Do you mind waiting a few minutes?"

"No problem." Jack's voice.

Callie straightened up fast, tugging the gaping side of her bodice close to her chest. He strolled into the room, all lean-hipped masculinity, enhanced by jeans that had been worn often enough to fit exactly how they should, and an open-necked shirt that was the perfect blend of tailored and casual.

"Doesn't Callie look beautiful?" Brenda prompted him.

He nodded at Callie, neither friendly nor hostile. "Seems like you're doing a great job with the dresses, Aunt Nancy."

His mouth curved into that smile that should come with a hazard warning. Callie added *too handsome* to the list of Jack Mitchell's failings. Even if Brenda got over her scruples about pressuring him to move closer to home, he would melt any objection with that smile.

Nancy beamed. "You're so sweet, Jack, I feel better just for seeing you."

Oh, please. As if he didn't already have a big enough opinion of his doctoring abilities.

"I don't know if I can take much credit for how good this dress looks on Callie," Nancy continued. "The color is gorgeous on her. All I need to do is fix this."

This turned out to be Callie's left breast; to her mortification, Nancy patted it. Jack followed the movement with interest.

"She means the dress needs adjusting there," Callie muttered.

"I wish your mom could be here to see how pretty you grew up," Brenda said, her voice shaky.

Instantly, Callie's throat clogged. She nodded, blinking hard.

Her mom, Jenny, had been best friends with Brenda in high school right here in Parkvale, until Jenny hitched a ride out of town after graduation. Years later, when leukemia forced her to give up wandering, Brenda had taken her and Callie into their home. There'd been an added bonus—Callie had clicked with Lucy Mitchell from the first minute and they'd become best friends, just like their moms. Peas in a pod, Brenda called them.

"Mom's right," Jack said quietly. "Jenny would be proud of you. On all counts." He touched Callie's arm, a gesture of understanding she hadn't expected. Her skin felt warm where his hand had made contact. He smiled again, a more intimate smile this time, that gave her just a glimpse of his perfect teeth.

Callie ran her tongue over her own now-perfect teeth. A couple of days after their wedding her mother had suggested she see an orthodontist. Her mom had liked Jack's teeth; she'd liked everything about him.

Maybe, on the inside, Jack was still that same decent guy. Callie's conviction that she'd been justified in lying to him ahead of his return to Parkvale wavered, and not just because he would soon discover her deception.

She shook off the twinge of guilt. Okay, Jack had displayed a moment's sensitivity. But that was far outweighed by eight years of his money-is-no-object-just-don't-ask-for-my-time philosophy. He sent expensive gifts from England at the right times, yet it seemed it was always the wrong time to pick up the phone.

"I'm coming out," Sarah announced from behind the curtain.

Aunt Nancy flapped her hands to gain the attention of the audience.

The bride emerged, stunning in a low-cut ivory silk dress. "Oooh," Nancy gasped, and started dabbing at her eyes with a tissue.

"Wow, cuz, you turned out not bad looking," Jack said.

Sarah stuck out her tongue. Then her eyes widened. "Uh…Aunt Brenda?"

Callie turned, and saw Brenda, white-faced, tears streaming down her cheeks.

"Mom," Jack said, alarmed.

Brenda waved her hands in front of her eyes. "Sorry…can't…stop…." The words came out as hiccuping sobs. Then she smiled—a deliberate clamping of the teeth, widening of the lips. "You look…so… beautiful."

Nancy offered her own damp tissue, patted her sister-in-law's shoulder. When Brenda didn't show any signs of drying up, a tangible unease rippled through the room.

At least the women felt it. Jack looked awkward, but not bothered. He probably thought women reacted like this all the time at the sight of a bride.

"Jack," Callie said sharply, "how about you take your mom home?"

He followed her cue. "Right. Let's go, Mom." He

led the still-weeping Brenda from the room while Callie raced to get changed. Nancy would have to adjust the left breast another day.

By the time she got out to the street, Brenda was in the Jaguar and had stopped crying. But her pallor was alarming.

Callie leaned in through the window. "Are you okay?"

"Oh, sweetie, you don't need to tell me I over-reacted in there." Brenda sounded her normal self. Only her white-knuckled grip on her purse revealed her stress.

"Hey, it was an emotional moment," Jack said from the driver's seat.

As if he knew the first thing about it! Brenda's tears were exactly the kind of change in behavior Callie had warned him about, and he'd chosen to ignore the heads-up. But now wasn't the time to argue. "Nancy will understand," she told Brenda.

Jack's mother bit her lip. "Nancy might," she said carefully, "but Dan won't."

"Huh?" Jack said.

"Dan might not hear," Callie said. But of course Nancy would tell Frank, and Frank would repeat it to his brother.

Brenda dropped her head back against the seat. "I must look a mess."

"You look fine," Jack assured her.

Honestly, the man had no idea! Callie hadn't wanted him back in town so he could humor his mom.

"I'd like to freshen up before we go home," Brenda told Callie.

"How about a cup of tea at the Eating Post?"

"Thank you." Brenda reached awkwardly to squeeze Callie's hand through the open window.

"So...we're going to the Eating Post?" Jack asked.

"That's right," Callie said. "I'll follow you in my car."

The restaurant was on the opposite side of Bicentennial Square from Fresher Flowers. Being Sunday, the place was deserted. Brenda headed straight to the bathroom; Callie led Jack to a table.

He slid into the other side of the booth from her. She drew a breath, and in the confined space, she inhaled him—soap and mint, the fresh-pressed cotton of his shirt, the scent of expensive leather. She sat back.

"Tell me why we're having tea," he said. "You and Mom were talking in code back there."

"To give your mother some time to pull herself together before she sees Dan."

He half laughed. "Dad's seen her upset before. I think he can handle it." He signaled to the waitress that they were ready to order.

"Dan doesn't like this kind of upset."

"It's the time of year," Jack said. "I'd expect them both to be a little tense."

"That's part of it," Callie admitted. Last week had been the anniversary of the day Lucy had drowned. She'd been swimming in the Tallee River during a school picnic. "There was certainly friction last year, but this year, your parents have been...stressed."

Jack looked skeptical. "Mom and Dad are rock solid."

Callie wanted to ask, *How would you know?* Instead, aware Brenda might return any moment, she forced herself to loosen her grip on the edge of the table.

"I didn't expect to see you at Nancy's house," she said conversationally. "I thought you'd be sleeping off your jet lag."

"Lying in bed staring at that mauve-and-magenta border was making me nauseous."

Callie tried hard not to imagine Jack lying in bed. Then she remembered it was *her* bed, when she was staying with Dan and Brenda. Casually, she ran the back of her hand over one cheek, then the other. Definitely warm. Probably red.

Jack leaned forward, his gaze assessing. "Are you okay? Do you have a fever?"

Good grief, did he have to try to diagnose her every reaction?

"I'm fine," she practically snapped. The only thing wrong with her was that she needed to spend less time talking to flowers and more time with living, breathing men, because her brain was still hung up on that bed thing.

He leaned in even farther to look at her, as if he could see right into the neural pathways of her mind.

Yikes. She eased away, thankful for the arrival of the waitress, and ordered tea for Brenda and herself. Jack asked for coffee.

When the woman left, he said abruptly, "You're mad at me."

"Excuse me?"

Jack had lain awake most of the night, due to a combination of jet lag and racing thoughts rather than lilac-paint-induced nausea. At 3:00 a.m., he'd turned his mind to Callie, and concluded that getting annoyed at her was counterproductive, given he needed her cooperation.

"I'm sorry I didn't recognize you at the shop," he said. No woman liked to think she was forgettable. He should have realized that earlier.

"You think I'd get mad about something like that?" She gave a toss of her nut-brown hair, which must have highlights in it, the way it caught the light and glinted gold where it touched her shoulders. "I took it as a compliment. I figured I'm a big improvement over the last time you saw me."

She was definitely ticked off. Unused to her brand of challenge—though he suspected he'd be getting used to it pretty fast—he drummed his fingers on the table. "If I say yes, I insult you as you were then, and if I say no, I'll insult you today."

"Which one's it going to be?" she asked.

Jack laughed, suddenly relaxing. Okay, so Callie was moody, but she was harmless. And funny. Diana, Jack's recently departed girlfriend, was a sophisticated, successful pediatrician, but she didn't have much of a sense of humor. Especially not about Jack's secret marriage.

Which brought him back to why he'd wanted to pick his mom up from this afternoon's dress fitting.

He'd completed the first item on his agenda: apologize for not recognizing Callie. He was willing to do number two, if necessary: soothe any feathers he might have ruffled by hogging the limelight with his parents. Jealousy was the other possible explanation for her snarkiness that had occurred to him in the middle of the night.

"How about we call a truce?" he said. Item number three.

Callie looked at him for a long moment, then nodded. "I don't want us to argue."

Even better, they were on the same wavelength. "Good," he said briskly. On to item number four. "We need to meet with a lawyer about the divorce. Can you make time tomorrow? And do you have anyone in mind?"

Her head bobbed at the change of subject. A frown put a little line above the bridge of her nose. "I don't think it's wise to see someone local. They're all members of Rotary and know your dad. I use a firm in Memphis for my loans. We could go there."

"Are they okay?"

She wrinkled her nose again, which somehow drew Jack's attention to her lips, full and pinky-red. "They're good value. And they're right across the road from my bank."

He tsked. "Imagine if people chose their doctor that way—cheap and handy to the bank."

"No one would do that. Doctors are *much* more important than lawyers." Her eyes were wide and innocent.

Jack was torn between amusement and exasperation. Callie had a mischievous streak a mile wide. Lucy would be the same, if she were still alive. He put the thought aside.

"I have a buddy in Memphis who had an irregular marriage situation," he said.

She snickered at his choice of words.

"I'll call him," Jack said, ignoring her. He saw his mom emerge from the restroom. "I'll find out who he used, set up a meeting."

"I'll leave it with you," Callie said.

Mission accomplished.

BY THE TIME THEY GOT Brenda home, there was no trace of tears. She confessed to Dan that she'd had "one of my turns, sweetie, but I'm all right now."

"Not again," Dan said. Callie wondered if Jack noticed that his father's impatience bordered on rudeness. And that Brenda's repeated apology had a take-it-or-leave-it-edge.

Callie left. Jack called later to say he'd arranged for them to meet his friend's lawyer in Memphis the next evening. For a guy who paid so little attention to his family, he was taking quite an active interest in their divorce.

The drive to Memphis took nearly three hours, so it would be a late night and Callie would have to close Fresher Flowers early, at four.

Closing early meant hustling her Monday afternoon regulars—a mother whose toddler loved to sniff the flowers; two elderly men; three women who circled the shop together complaining about the prices—out the door before they were ready.

As she tried to shepherd them out without being rude, Jack pulled up in the black Jaguar. He got out of the car, frowning when he saw the Open sign in her window.

Callie frowned back.

He observed the departing shoppers' empty hands. "Did any of those people buy anything?"

"Not this time." Callie brushed at the lily pollen on her skirt, even though experience told her she needed to lift it off with sticky tape, then hang the skirt out in the sun. Predictably, the yellow streaks didn't budge from the white cotton. "I get a few people coming here because they find flowers restful, or the scent brings back memories," she said. "And those old men...I think they're lonely."

"So is bankruptcy. There was no one in here last time I came, either."

"*You* were here and you spent a hundred dollars," she said acerbically. "As far as I'm concerned your money's as welcome as anyone else's."

Jack held up his hands in a butting-out gesture. "What do we need to do to get out of here?" *Oh, yeah, we're having a truce.*

Together, they brought in the tubs of flowers from outside. Jack's clothing was immaculate, his jeans and long-sleeved, bronze-colored polo shirt fitting as if custom-made, but he didn't seem concerned about the threat of pollen or other dirt. Callie chalked up a small point in his favor. His thick dark hair and chiseled cheekbones, on the other hand, were not pluses. They only encouraged women to fawn over him. When she got married for real, Callie thought, *if* she got married for real, she'd never find a guy as good-looking—her shallow side felt a pang of regret—but at least she'd find someone unselfish.

Jack waited while she locked up, then held the car door open for her.

The Jaguar was every bit as luxurious as it looked. Virtually no engine noise penetrated the interior; Jack pressed a button on the console and Norah Jones wafted through discreetly located speakers.

As they pulled away from the lights at the intersection of Main and Fifth, Callie waved to a group of men. One of them waved back.

"Who was that?" Jack asked.

She rolled her eyes. "Your cousin Jason."

"Thought so."

"With his brother, also your cousin."

"Excellent guys," he said.

"So excellent that you don't remember what they look like from one day to the next."

"Hey, I didn't get a more than a glimpse of them just now."

Callie cautioned herself against launching into Jack with an accusation that he hadn't recognized his family because he didn't give a damn about anyone in Parkvale. *Truce,* she reminded herself again. She'd bet money he liked being criticized even less than most people. So when she said her piece tonight, she'd do it without yelling.

She pressed her lips together as Jack turned right and joined the interstate. She adjusted her seat, tested the smoothness of the leather upholstery with her fingers, then checked the glove compartment. Empty. She fiddled with the climate control for her side of the car. Cool air fanned her face, lifting her hair. She flipped the visor down to check if her hair was mussed. Hmm, not the best… She combed her fingers through it.

"Are you ADHD?" Jack asked.

Callie froze midcomb. "Will you stop doing that?"

"What?"

She dropped her hands into her lap. "Stop suggesting there's something wrong with me every time I pull a face or scratch my nose."

"I don't." He sounded genuinely surprised.

"Sometimes a squint is just a squint and a scratch is just a scratch."

"I'm a doctor. I notice these things." He was using his calming-a-crazy-patient tone again.

"And stop talking in that irritating voice."

"You mean this one?" he said soothingly.

She reached across and smacked his arm. Encountering solid muscle beneath his polo shirt, she whipped her hand away. Neurosurgery must be a lot more physical than she thought.

He looked down at his arm, where she'd touched him, then glanced sidelong at her. "ADHD might explain—"

"Stop," she ordered. "You don't have to be a doctor every minute of the day."

He frowned. "Of course I do. You can't tell me you haven't noticed what those are." He waved at the variegated-leaved, deep red wildflowers growing alongside the interstate.

"Trilliums, Sweet Betsy variety," she said automatically. "Common throughout the state."

"See? If you can be a florist every minute of the day, I can be a doctor." He paused. "So...no ADHD? Just a bad case of the fidgets?"

"I was keeping myself *occupied* so I wouldn't get mad at you."

He rubbed his chin. "You're mad about me not recognizing my cousins?" His tone suggested there was no end to her unreasonableness.

"Yes…no…it's more than that." Callie chewed her lip, wondering where to start.

"We're having a truce," he reminded her.

"The only reason I'm holding back."

He laughed. "Let's talk about something that won't make you mad. How's the flower business?"

She twisted to face him. "Are you planning on offering more advice?"

"I have a responsibility to make sure you're financially stable before we divorce."

"Excuse me?"

"I promised your mother." He didn't sound as if he was kidding.

"I'm twenty-five," Callie said. "Mom wouldn't expect you to worry about me now."

That was met with silence.

"I'm the *least* of your responsibilities." A tiny dig she didn't count as breaking their truce.

"Humor me," he said, "and tell me how you're doing. As soon as we get this divorce, you're on your own."

Callie shivered.

"You can turn the air down if you're cold." He adjusted the dial on her side.

He was doing it again. Callie's fingers curled on her knees.

"I can't figure out if you suffer from a total lack of sensitivity," she said, "or if diagnosing a physical cause for every action comes with the high-handed, I-know-best doctor territory."

With exaggerated care, he turned the temperature dial back up again. "If this is truce talk," he said, "I'm glad we're not fighting."

Callie bared her teeth at him; it couldn't be called a smile, but stopped short of a snarl.

Jack, on the other hand, did smile. "So, your finances. I assume your mom didn't leave you much?"

"Her insurance was just enough to cover my orthodontist bills," Callie said. Sensing his surprise, she added defensively, "At the time, it seemed good use of the money."

Another of those sideways glances from Jack. She almost covered her mouth with her hand, the way she used to before her teeth were straightened. Talking about the past made her feel like that awkward seventeen-year-old again.

"Then, what, there was no money left for college?" He flipped his turn signal and zipped past a Winnebago.

"I got a one-year business diploma at community college, mostly paid for by your parents," she said. "Even if there'd been the money for college, I would have chosen to stay in Parkvale." In the interests of their truce, she kept any comparison with his leave-and-don't-look-back attitude out of her voice.

"I guess you would, given the lengths we went to so you could stay with my folks," he said, equally neutrally.

Callie relaxed. If they stayed on their best behavior, she could envisage them having a mature discussion about Dan and Brenda. The kind of discussion they should have had years ago, if only she'd been able to dump the image of Jack as the authoritative figure who'd made all the decisions, starting with their wedding.

"Do you realize," she said, "the last time I traveled in a car with you was on our wedding day?"

CHAPTER THREE

JACK STARED STRAIGHT through the windshield. "You were a nervous wreck. I didn't think you'd go through with it."

"You had enough confidence for both of us," Callie said.

"Did I?" His face was inscrutable.

"So did Mom. It was the last big decision she made."

By then, Jenny had been fighting leukemia for two years. And for six months, she'd been fighting a losing battle with her ex-husband's parents, who'd petitioned for custody of sixteen-year-old Callie the moment they'd heard about Jenny's illness. They'd also lodged a claim for immediate temporary custody on the basis her mom could no longer look after her.

Jenny's own parents had died years earlier, and she was determined those wicked people, as she called her in-laws, would never have custody of her daughter. Callie had been equally determined not to go to her unknown grandparents. Parkvale, and more specifically Dan and Brenda Mitchell's home, was the first proper home she'd known. Besides, her mother had needed her, and Callie had needed to stay with her mom until the end.

"But you weren't convinced getting married was the right decision," Jack suggested, bringing her back to the moment.

"I didn't have any better ideas," she hedged. She pointed to a police car up ahead; he nodded and eased off the gas. "I couldn't think at all, what with Mom moving into long-stay hospital care…and then Lucy drowning."

Jack, home from Boston for his sister's funeral, had been accepted for postgraduate study at Oxford University. Brenda was already upset at the thought of him being so far away. After Lucy's death, she was distraught.

It was Jack who'd come up with the brilliant idea that if Callie married him, which she could legally do with her mother's permission, she would be beyond the reach of the Summers's custody suit. Brenda and Dan would continue to have Callie, Lucy's best friend and someone they doted on.

And Jack could escape, worry-free, to England.

"You have to admit, we were…underhanded," Callie said.

He shifted his grip on the steering wheel. "We couldn't have told Mom and Dad. They're so hung up on the sanctity of marriage, there's no way they'd have condoned it. And Mom wasn't well."

Brenda had plunged into a black depression when Lucy died. Only the routines of her normal life—which for her meant lavishing care on Dan and Callie—kept her going.

Jack was right. Keeping the wedding a secret had been the right thing to do—then and now.

Callie's mom had been allowed out of the hospital for

a couple of hours for the wedding, and the three of them traveled to the chapel in Jack's beat-up Mustang. He'd presented Callie with a corsage—a pink rose, with baby's breath. Unimaginative, but she'd thought it beautiful.

If she closed her eyes she could still smell that rose.

She'd literally been shaking from nerves. Jack had taken her hand, with nothing remotely sexual in his touch, and steadied her.

If the marriage celebrant thought there was anything odd about a handsome, assured doctor marrying a tongue-tied, gap-toothed schoolgirl, he didn't show it. The ceremony took minutes, and afterward, Jenny cried tears of relief.

"It's too late to regret our wedding now," Jack said. "You need to think about your future. Is the flower business where you want to be long term?"

"I like the independence, being my own boss," she said. "When I started Fresher Flowers nearly a year ago I'd been working at that store by the hospital for three years. I kept thinking I could do a better job than my boss."

Jack nodded.

"The day I decided I could no longer stand seeing work that was less than perfect go out the door, I quit to go it alone."

"Wasn't that risky? It seems to be a competitive industry these days."

She shrugged. "I travel up to Memphis at least a couple of mornings a week for the flower auction. It gives me an edge over my rivals, who mainly buy from wholesalers."

"Do you own the building?"

"I rent, but I paid for the refit. With my money, not yours."

She'd borrowed money from Jack five years ago to fund the down payment on her first house. After she'd renovated, buying her materials at cost from Dan's hardware store, she'd sold the house and channeled part of the profit into the next one, part into her savings. Then repeated the pattern several times. The last two houses, she'd used all her own money. The shop refit had come out of her savings. She didn't like to think how precarious that left her, but she couldn't keep borrowing from Jack.

"You still use me as security for your mortgage, right?" he asked.

"Uh-huh. One look at your supersurgeon income and a loan officer is putty in my hands." There was no risk to him, because she only bought properties she could acquire for below market value.

"Will our divorce make it harder for you to get a loan?"

She eyed his hands on the steering wheel— surgeon's hands with long, tapered fingers. No rings. Just like hers.

"I'll manage." At their wedding, she'd worn her mother's ring, then returned it to Jenny. It had come back to her in the plastic bag of her mother's personal effects. Callie had put it in a box in her lingerie drawer, along with a shark-tooth pendant that had reportedly belonged to her father. She suspected Jenny had bought the pendant to give her some souvenir of the drifter dad who'd drifted away for good when she was eight.

Jack frowned as he downshifted to pass a semi-trailer. The truck was an enormous red blur alongside the car. "I could continue to back your loans, I suppose."

"Once the shop is doing better, it'll serve as security," Callie said. "I won't need you."

He pounced. "The business isn't doing well?"

"It's a start-up. These things take time."

Jack drummed his fingers on the steering wheel. "If you got married again you'd be more secure."

She drew herself up in the seat. "You don't think I can make a go of the shop?"

"Not if you see it as a hangout for the poor and lonely. You don't want to get married?" he asked, mimicking her tone.

"To someone I love, sure," she replied. "Not to get a bank loan."

"Do you have a boyfriend?" Jack said, as if the possibility had only just occurred to him. As if she were chopped liver.

"I still see Rob sometimes," she said coolly.

He frowned. "Rob?"

"Rob Hanson, the guy I was dating when we got married."

Jack's head jerked around. "I don't remember that you were dating anyone."

"Are you kidding?" Callie said. "I was crazy about him. As in love as only a teenager can be."

He snorted. But he shifted in his seat, as if the news discomfited him.

"We dated for three years," she said with relish. "Then we got engaged."

Jack's foot hit the brake, jolting the car. Instinctively, he flung out an arm to protect Callie as he fumbled for the gas pedal. He accidentally smacked into the softness of her breasts.

"Sorry," he muttered, concentrating on keeping the car straight in the lane. Behind him, someone honked. Dammit, if he crashed this thing it would be her fault. He waved an apology to the other driver, brought the car back up to eighty. "How could you get engaged when you were married?" he demanded.

"We planned a long engagement." She rubbed a hand across her breasts where he'd touched her; Jack tried not to look. "I figured you and I would have gotten around to a divorce by the time Rob and I set a wedding date."

"Quite the juggling act." The comment came out surly, which didn't make sense. He cleared his throat. "I'm surprised Brenda didn't tell you I was engaged."

"I don't always get time to read every word of her e-mails," he admitted.

Callie's lips clamped together in a thin line that suggested considerable self-restraint.

"Did you say you're still with, uh, Rob?" Jack asked.

She shook her head. "I broke off the engagement after a year. Four years ago."

"Why?"

She didn't answer. The hum of the tires against the pavement changed its rhythm as they started across a bridge. Callie looked out the window. Below them, the Mississippi River flowed high and fast, fed by the spring rains.

"Was he ugly?" Jack prompted.

"He's very good-looking."

"Dumb?"

"He's not a brain surgeon, but he's smart. Not arrogant," she added, her meaning only too clear. "Rob's a great guy. Anyone would be lucky to have him."

"Except you."

"We get along well, we go out sometimes."

Jack looked across at her, and noticed her white skirt had ridden up to show an alluringly smooth length of thigh.

Something tugged inside him...something elemental that wasn't on the list of appropriate feelings for Callie.

He banished it, disentangled his thoughts. He did *not* want to know exactly how much of each other she and Rob saw.

Then she ran her tongue across her lower lip and it was—dammit—it was *sexy.*

Appalled, Jack wrenched his gaze away. He needed to see her only as Callie, bratty kid sister, to keep this whole process simple.

Damn.

CALLIE WAS ASKING HERSELF for the thousandth time why she hadn't gone ahead and married Rob, when she realized Jack had stopped coming up with helpful suggestions about how she should live, and had fallen silent.

It must be her turn to interfere in his life. Of course, she'd be more tactful than he was.

"A career like yours must make it hard to find time for meaningful relationships."

Jack's eyes narrowed; he wasn't buying it. "I shouldn't have stuck my nose into your love life, and I'm sorry."

"I'm talking about your parents."

He slowed the car as the traffic grew heavier. They were near Memphis now. "I admit I get busy, but I keep in regular contact."

Was he deluded or lying? Callie decided not to use the word *neglect,* because that sounded negative. Ditto for *abandon, selfish* and *uncaring.* Where was the guy who'd squeezed her arm in comfort when she'd developed a bad case of shivers after their wedding? Who'd laughed out loud when she'd blurted an ancient Doctor, Doctor joke to lighten the moment? His kindness had convinced her everything would be okay. As okay as it could be.

Stick with the facts, the way a doctor would. "When you called to say you were coming home, they hadn't heard from you in two months—that was just a quick e-mail—and before that it was a five-minute phone call three months earlier."

An ominous silence filled the car. "Did Mom complain to you?"

"She would never criticize you."

"Maybe you should take a leaf out of her book." The reasonable words had an acid edge. "Because if she's happy…"

With a finger, she traced the scalloped hem of her skirt over her thighs, saw his gaze dart in the direction of the movement. "They're not getting any younger," she persisted.

"They're not old, either. Mom's fifty-seven—"

"Fifty-eight," she corrected.

"Which makes Dad sixty. They're in good health. Right now, my patients need me a lot more than my parents need to hear about the weather in Oxford."

Callie recalled the way Brenda made self-deprecating excuses for her son's lack of contact, and her pride when she relayed whatever scant information he deigned to share. "I'm not talking about physical health. Or did you not have time to 'read every word' of my e-mails?"

"You mean that bunch of cryptic communications that took two thousand words to say Mom 'isn't herself'?"

Callie drew in a long, slow breath. When this conversation was over, she'd have qualified for sainthood on the grounds of a miracle of forbearance. "I know your time is valuable. But so is everyone's."

"Very true," he said. "Arranging flowers, performing brain surgery—there's only so much we can fit into our days."

She nobly refrained from calling him on his arrogance, and pressed on. "But while you're in Parkvale you won't have those pressures. So maybe you could take time to find out why she's so down."

"*If* she is," he said.

Callie didn't rise to that. "You know it's her birthday on the fifteenth, right?"

"Of course," he said, too easily.

Callie telegraphed her disbelief.

He grinned, but he didn't back down. "I'll order a

special bouquet from Fresher Flowers for the occasion."

"You know what she'd like more than flowers?"

"Yes."

Callie blinked. "You do?"

"You're going to say half an hour of my time, or something else that makes me look mean."

She bit back on a smile. "She'd love for you to take her shopping."

"You mean, to choose a gift?"

Callie shrugged. "Not necessarily. Brenda always runs into at least thirty people she knows when she's out shopping. She'd get to show you off."

"I'm not a prize exhibit," he muttered, irritated.

Callie folded her arms across her chest. "The limited sightings of you over the past several years convinced me you're a rare species."

"I may not have been in Parkvale, but I'm always only a phone call or a flight away." His voice was tighter now.

"You mean in case of a medical emergency?"

"I didn't mean for a shopping emergency."

"Your folks aren't sick, but I think your mother is close to her emotional breaking point."

Jack paused. "That diagnosis seems a little extreme. If there's anything seriously wrong, believe me, I'll see it." He switched into the right lane, ready to exit the interstate. "But, Callie…" he flashed her the smile she suspected was calculated to make her roll over to have her tummy tickled "…I really appreciate your concern, and I know Mom and Dad do, too."

His crazy-patient voice was back.

THEY ARRIVED IN Germantown, an affluent part of Memphis, at seven, and pulled up outside a solid three-story Georgian-style house.

Callie shook herself out of her contemplation of Jack's arrogant denial that she might have a better handle on his parents than he did. "What's this guy's name again?"

"Sam Magill. His wife is my friend Adam Carmichael's stepmother."

"Adam Carmichael, the TV network guy?"

He nodded. "His family owns Memphis Channel Eight—do you know him?"

"A few years back, a girl from Parkvale—Casey Greene, whose sister Karen is one of my best friends—conned her fiancé into a surprise wedding show on Channel Eight. The guy dumped her on air and she ended up marrying Adam Carmichael in a fake wedding. Only it turned out to be legit."

"None of that makes the slightest sense." When Jack said things like that, his voice held a hint of a British accent that in other circumstances Callie might have found appealing.

"Casey and Adam must be the 'irregular marriage situation' you were talking about," she said.

He pulled the key from the ignition. "If Sam dealt with the mess you just described, our divorce will be a piece of cake."

The tall, slim woman who opened the wide front door was in her late fifties and extremely stylish.

"I'm Eloise Magill. You must be Callie." She gave Callie's hand a sympathetic squeeze. "And you must be Jack." Her tone was cool, as if whatever was wrong with their marriage had to be his fault. Callie decided she liked Eloise.

"Sam's just finishing a phone call." She led them into a living room where the décor was an eclectic mix of chunky masculine furniture and feminine fripperies. Leather couches flanked a pink-and-gray-striped love seat; a silk fan, beaded glass coasters and a copy of *Vogue* cluttered the solid wooden coffee table. Somehow, it worked.

Sam, who had eyebrows bushy enough to house a small colony of beetles, and punctuated his telephone conversation with a startling smoker's cough, acknowledged them with a wave.

A moment later, he hung up. "Thanks for looking after my guests, darling." He took Eloise's hand for a moment, then reluctantly relinquished it. The way he looked at her, and the way she looked right back, suggested this couple would never need a divorce lawyer.

Callie put a few more inches between her and Jack. Sam shook hands with them, directed them to one of the two leather couches, and sat down opposite. Eloise left the room with a promise to bring coffee.

"Why don't you two tell me your situation?" Sam unscrewed the cap of his pen. "Then we can work out how best to proceed."

Jack relaxed into the couch. He liked the look of Sam, and his calm logic. Even better, Callie had gone unexpectedly quiet. For the first time since he'd landed back in the U.S.A., he felt as if he was making progress toward the purpose of this trip.

He outlined to Sam how and why they'd got married. Even keeping it to the bare bones, the story didn't get any better with the telling. He had a sudden inkling why Diana, his ex-girlfriend, had been so shocked to learn the truth, and why the gossip had spread so mercilessly among his colleagues.

"And now you want a divorce," Sam said mildly, as if the end to this charade wasn't long overdue. He tapped his pen against his legal pad. "Normally I'd recommend a husband and wife seek separate representation."

"It's not a proper marriage," Jack said. "We both want to end it, as soon as possible." He glanced at Callie for corroboration, but she was staring down at her hands, her cheeks sucked in as if she might start carping on about his parents again if she opened her mouth the tiniest bit.

It was probably best she didn't talk.

Sam flipped his pen between his fingers. "My first duty as your lawyer is to recommend that you attempt to resolve your differences through mediation."

"We barely know each other. We don't *have* differences." Jack discounted the disagreement they'd had in the car, which had been pretty tame. Beside him, Callie's fingers twitched.

Sam nodded. "Okay, you're waiving mediation. Next, you need to consider that under Tennessee law, the default position is an equitable division of the matrimonial property."

Callie perked up. "Do neurosurgeons earn more than florists?" she asked brightly. "I mean, I know they're a lot more *important*."

Jack shot her a look, one that worked well to crush know-it-all medical residents. She was entirely uncrushed. Her blue eyes sparked the way they had the day he'd arrived in town. *Ignore her*.

"We've agreed we'll each take out of the marriage what we brought into it," he told the lawyer.

Sam raised his eyebrows at Callie, who sighed theatrically, then nodded. The lawyer pursed his lips, and Jack was pretty sure the man was stifling a smile.

So much for their truce. Jack gritted his teeth. He'd gone easy on Callie in the car when she'd hassled him about his parents. Big mistake. Now she thought she could mess him around. He shouldn't have given in to that unexpected sense of guilt that he might have exploited her desperate situation all those years ago.

"I'll prepare the paperwork you'll both need to sign in order to waive your share of your spouse's assets," Sam said. "Now, have a look at this." He held out a sheet of paper, which Callie took before Jack could. "It's a list of the permissible grounds for divorce in Tennessee. You'll need to choose one."

Jack refused to crane his neck to see over Callie's shoulder. He could wait.

She made a show of tapping her chin with a finger, apparently deep in contemplation, then pointed to an item high on the list. "I like this first one. 'Either party is naturally impotent and incapable of procreation.'" She jerked her head in Jack's direction and gave Sam a significant look.

Jack clenched his teeth, but by superhuman effort refrained from declaring to Sam that he was *not* impotent. Because on that subject, there was such a thing as protesting too much. Still, he couldn't hold back a growl.

Callie patted his knee. "Sweetie, it's nothing to be ashamed of."

A muffled sound came from Sam.

Okay, Jack was going to throttle her. Not here in the lawyer's house; that would be stupid. He'd do it after they left, somewhere near the airport, where he could jump on the next plane before they found her body. The prospect of such utter abandonment of his Hippocratic oath cheered him.

"You know," Callie reflected, "I'm thinking 'willful or malicious desertion or absence without a reasonable cause' might be more appropriate."

He looked down his nose at her. "I don't think any judge will consider my commitment to saving children's lives unreasonable."

"Touché," she said sadly, and read on. "'Cruel and inhuman treatment,'" she murmured with interest. "Oh, wait, I guess they mean toward me, not your parents."

Jack snatched the list from her and began reading. "Here we go," he said, triumphant. "All I have to do is make an attempt on your life, 'by poison or any other means—' and we have guaranteed grounds for divorce."

She put a hand to her throat, as if she'd sensed the modus operandi of her imminent demise. "Go ahead. Your parents will see more of you when you're in jail than they do now."

She was driving him nuts. Jack turned away, so he wouldn't be tempted to respond. "Do we need to decide the grounds now?" he asked Sam. "What's the time line on this thing? I know we have to wait until I've been here thirty days before we can file."

Oh, heck. Callie dragged air into her suddenly constricted lungs. She'd known her lie would come out, but she'd rather it wasn't right after she'd been goading Jack. Was there any chance Sam wouldn't expose her?

The lawyer's shaggy eyebrows shot up. She was dead in the water.

"That's not right," Sam said. "As long as you have grounds, which it seems you do on several counts, and as long as one of you has been resident in Marquette County the past six months—" he looked at Callie, who reluctantly nodded "—and you've lived apart for a continuous period of two or more years without cohabiting as man and wife during that period..." He took a breath as he finished the spiel, then sealed Callie's fate. "You can file the papers tomorrow." He spread his hands. "Your divorce will be through in sixty days."

"You mean," Jack said slowly. "I have to stay for sixty days from when we file?"

Sam shook his head. "You don't need to stay—in fact, you don't have to be here at all. Callie can file for the divorce."

Callie sucked in her cheeks and tried to appear surprised.

But Dr. Megabrain, who more often than not talked to her as if she had a whole bunch of screws missing, didn't consider for one second that she might have misunderstood the Tennessee Code.

He twisted on the couch. Anger darkened his eyes to gunmetal, and he aimed an accusing finger at her jugular. "You lied to me."

CHAPTER FOUR

"YOU'D ALREADY DECIDED to come home." Callie tried out the smooth, crazy-patient voice and was delighted to see it riled him every bit as much as it did her. "I just exaggerated the length of time you'd need to be here."

Sam tutted.

Jack snapped his teeth shut. "I came back because I wanted to make sure you were okay, like I *promised your mom*. You had no right to turn this into your agenda."

But Callie was done feeling guilty. She wasn't the one neglecting the two most wonderful parents in the world. She jabbed a finger right back at him. "If I hadn't said you needed to be here a month, you'd have flown in, checked up on me, spent two days with your parents, then left again."

The flicker in his eyes told her she was right. But her satisfaction was short-lived, shriveling in the heat of his rising fury.

"What will it take for you to understand that I'm not in England because I think it's more *fun* than Parkvale? There are people, patients—kids—whose lives depend on me." He jerked to his feet as if he could no longer bear to share the expanse of leather with her. "Okay, so sometimes that means I have less time available for my family. But other families—my patients' families—would say it's a sacrifice worth making. Who gave you the right to interfere?"

She couldn't believe he hadn't figured that out yet. "*You* gave me the right, you pompous, egotistical...neurosurgeon! You left me here to take your place, comforting your parents after Lucy died—don't you dare deny it," she ordered, as he opened his mouth.

Of course he ignored her. "You're twisting the truth," he barked. "I didn't want my mom and dad to lose you so soon after Lucy."

"You were worried your mom would pressure you not to go to Oxford. If I was there in your place, you could leave the country and forget Dan and Brenda."

"I knew Mom would be *happier* about me leaving if you—"

"You *used* me so you could quit your family when your parents needed you most," she retorted. "Don't try and tell me your years in England have been any kind of sacrifice. You wanted out, and you got it."

"That's not true," he roared down at her.

She slapped the arm of the couch in frustration, then stood in a futile attempt to level the playing field. Everything about him was bigger, stronger, more powerful than she was. "You don't visit, you hardly ever phone. Sure, you play the generous son and fly your parents to see you every so often, but you barely take a day off work to be with them."

He paled, and she momentarily regretted letting

slip the nearest thing to criticism Brenda had said about her son. Callie shored up her flagging defenses. "You don't bother to read the e-mails that might give you a clue what's going on here."

Sam cleared his throat. "Perhaps the mediation I mentioned earlier..." he began.

Jack ignored the lawyer.

"I see the important stuff," he said dismissively.

She snapped her fingers. "I don't mean things like your dad's blood pressure spikes—"

"Since when does Dad have high blood pressure?"

"His *doctor* deals with that," she said. She'd obviously been too subtle in her e-mails. "I'm talking about your mom's midlife crisis, and your parents' marriage breakdown."

He gaped. "Mom's not having a midlife crisis. She's not the type."

Okay, could somebody hand her a sledgehammer?

"And Mom and Dad's marriage is not breaking down," he added. "I haven't seen anything beyond normal *tension*—" the word she'd used in her e-mails "—between them."

"You don't *want* to see, in case it complicates your Very Important Life."

"That's garbage. I'll talk to Dad about his blood pressure, but beyond that..."

"This isn't an extended house call," she said, beyond frustrated. "It's your family. Look deeper, Jack."

He turned away abruptly, rejecting everything she'd said.

"You've changed," she accused. "You used to be so kind, so caring."

"You used to be so quiet," he retorted.

Just like that, Callie ran out of steam. She sagged onto the couch, back against the cushions, breathing hard.

"Those grounds for divorce," Sam mused in his gravelly voice, "I'm thinking irreconcilable differences."

FROM THE WAY JACK STRODE out of the Magills' house, Callie half expected him to jump in the Jaguar and roar off without her.

With his long legs, he could have beaten her to the car easily. But when he hit the steps, he stopped. The porch light threw the planes of his cheeks into sharp relief, illuminated a slow, satisfied smile. What was that about?

He continued down the wide steps. By the time he reached the bottom, Callie was right beside him. She discerned a spring in his step and…was he *whistling* under his breath?

Deeply suspicious—even more so when he held the car door open for her with a slight bow—she slid into her seat.

After about a mile of driving in silence, broken only by the sound of Callie's stomach growling—she had said all she could without losing her temper, and Jack was preoccupied—he pulled into the parking lot of a Happy Burgers restaurant. He positioned the Jaguar precisely between a Ford Bronco and a Toyota Corolla, and buzzed his window closed. "You're hungry, let's eat."

Typical. He was deciding once again what was wrong with her and what she should do about it.

"Didn't they teach you in medical school that junk food is bad for you?" Callie's stomach growled again. She pressed a hand to her middle.

"I don't want to listen to that all the way back," he said, and got out of the car.

"I hope you're good at treating indigestion," she called as she stomped across the lot behind him.

Inside, Jack ordered a large fries and two giant burgers for himself plus a Coke to wash them down. Callie had planned on ordering a salad, but the smell of grease and carbs seduced her into a cheeseburger and fries. And a caramel sundae—that plastic-tasting sticky sauce was irresistible.

"This'll probably kill me," she grumbled as they sat down.

"I can only hope," he said cheerfully. He nudged her tray farther onto the molded plastic table, which hadn't been wiped since the last customer.

Callie refused to put her food on the table, but Jack reached around to deposit his tray on the waste station behind him. He set his burger down, heedless of marauding bacteria, and ignored Callie as he unwrapped his food. He looked happier than he had since he'd arrived in Parkvale, which made no sense.

"That meeting was a total disaster." She sucked the salt off a French fry. "Sam must think we're psychos."

Jack chomped a mouthful of burger. "He thought you were a psycho, for sure. I think he recognized a fellow professional in me."

"By the way you threatened to kill me?"

He grinned. Now she was seriously worried.

"I'm still thinking about claiming you're impotent," she said, trying to bait him.

He regarded her blandly. "You do what you have to."

Callie had the horrible sense that her chances of convincing him to help his parents were slithering away. She tried a new tack. "Jack, I'm sorry I exaggerated—"

"Lied."

"—about how long you need to be here."

He shrugged. "Doesn't matter."

"It's just that I care a lot about your folks, so I…" She stopped, burger halfway to her mouth. "What do you mean, it doesn't matter?"

He leaned back in the booth, arms folded across his chest. "Are you forgetting what I learned in our meeting with Sam?"

Had she missed something? Desperately, she cast her mind back. "That impotence is nothing to be ashamed of?"

His mouth firmed into a hard, straight line. He planted his palms on the table and leaned forward. "That I don't need to be here for us to get a divorce. I'm going back to England."

"You can't!"

"You can't," he echoed. "Stop me." He popped several fries into his mouth.

Callie's burger sank like a stone in her stomach. "But your parents—"

"Will understand I need to get back to my patients. I'll make sure Dad's doctor is on top of his blood pressure. I'll even ask Mom if she needs any help," he said with exaggerated generosity. "I figure I can wrap up this visit by Wednesday, Thursday tops."

He couldn't do that. Except his supreme confidence assured her he could. Callie grabbed for something, anything, that would keep him here. "Back when you were pretending to be a decent guy, you said you wanted to make sure I'm secure, to keep your promise to my mom. You haven't done that."

He drank some of his Coke. "You have your business, you own a house, you have my parents eating out of your hand, and you're willing to lie and manipulate people to get what you want. I'd say you're doing a damn good job of looking after yourself."

Her throat suddenly dry, Callie swallowed.

"Callie," he said, "my patients need me. I had a call from one of my colleagues just this morning asking if I'm available to perform a difficult craniectomy."

"No one's indispensable. They're covering for you at the moment."

"But I'm the best," he said.

"You expect me to believe you care that much for your patients, yet so little for your parents?"

"I love my parents," he said. "And they are *my* parents. You're just going to have to trust me to make the right choices."

"Like you did eight years ago?" she flared.

She'd set a match to Jack's guilt again, and he couldn't tamp it down as easily as he'd like. He and her mom hadn't given her any real choice, he could see that now. It had crossed his mind years ago that the other way to circumvent her grandparents' custody suit would be to help her apply for emancipation as a minor. But emancipation would have taken longer, would have been open to challenge by her grandparents. It had been riskier from her mother's perspective…and from his.

Jack made up his mind. "Our marriage achieved its aims, so, yes, it was the right decision."

Saying it aloud, so unequivocally, made it *feel* right. The guilt fizzled out to nothing. He had an incredible opportunity ahead of him at work. He wouldn't let anything derail him. Not hindsight, not Parkvale and especially not Callie.

"Even if getting married was the right thing at the time," she said, "it's not anymore. I'm not enough for Brenda, I'm not her daughter. Lucy's gone. And now so are you."

He balled his burger wrapper. "My parents are adults who are quite capable of working out their own problems. If they have any. Which they don't."

Callie clutched her head.

He ignored her. "If Sam doesn't have the papers waiving our matrimonial property rights ready by the time I leave, he can send them to England and I'll sign." He demolished a third of the burger in one bite. "Of course, you don't need me to sign the actual divorce petition," he said around his mouthful.

Callie pushed her sundae away, which Jack considered a waste of good food, so he nabbed it. She had a tiny splodge of vanilla soft-freeze on her chin; he reached across, wiped it away with his index finger. Her chin even *felt* stubborn.

She jerked her head aside. "Leave me alone."

"You had ice-cream on your chin." He held up the finger to show her.

"I won't do it."

"Excuse me?"

She squared her shoulders. "I won't sign the divorce petition."

For a second, he froze. Then he relaxed. "No

problem, I'll sign it. As long as one of us has been resident here, it doesn't matter who files for divorce. And we qualify on just about all grounds." His eyes narrowed. "Except impotence."

"I'll contest the divorce."

"You can't contest irreconcilable differences." Jack heard the uncertainty in his own voice.

"Yes, I can—and that's not all I can do. My friend Karen, the one whose sister married your friend Adam, is a lawyer. When Karen's husband tried to divorce her on the same grounds, she asked the judge to order them both to attend counseling for a month."

It seemed it was Callie's turn to sit back and fold her arms. Static electricity charged her brown hair, fanning it across the booth's vinyl seatback, the way it might fan out on a pillow.

Jack waved a hand dismissively. "I'm not doing any counseling."

"I want you to stay the full month," Callie said, "so you can see how bad things are for your mom, and help her. I'm lodging a petition for counseling tomorrow."

"Go ahead. I'll be gone by Thursday."

The serene smile she mustered was fake. This was last-ditch time. "I doubt the judge will appreciate you skipping town right after you've been ordered to attend counseling. You might find our divorce gets turned down."

Jack stilled. If he didn't go back to England with that divorce in hand, his bosses would reconsider sending him on the Paris exchange he'd been angling for.

"This is nuts," he growled.

"Stay here a month, and I'll sign the divorce pap[er]
along with you," she replied.

Jack drummed his fingers on the table as he c[on-]
sidered his options. He could apply for a divorce [in]
England, but he had no idea what was involved. A[nd]
the Brits didn't exactly move fast, he'd found. "Fi[ne,]"
he said, though it wasn't. "I'll stay the month, if y[ou]
sign the damn papers this week."

"I don't trust you not to figure out some w[ay]
around it."

"You're calling *me* a liar now? As well as pomp[ous]
and egotistical?" He fired the words she'd used at [the]
Magills' house.

Guilt, or maybe embarrassment, flickered on [her]
face. Then she said, "Who knew a guy could be s[uch]
a jerk and still have his parents convinced he'[s a]
saint?"

His low rumble of anger startled her. She sto[od,]
picked up her tray. "You never know," she said. "[You]
might even benefit from some relationship couns[el-]
ing."

"We don't have a relationship," he snarled, los[ing]
all pretense at calm. At the next table, a young mot[her]
glared at him.

Callie sniffed, managed to look teary-ey[ed.]
"Sweetie, you know it upsets me when you say th[at."]

The young woman called out to Callie, "Divo[rce]
him, honey."

"You heard her," Jack said.

Callie shook her head. Jack clenched his hands [on]
the table, but she wasn't worried. She was confid[ent]

he wasn't the violent sort...which was just as well, because right now he looked mad enough to grab a scalpel and remove a few of her vital organs. "I'll sign the papers at the end of the month."

"Or I could just kill you tonight and save myself a lot of trouble," he muttered.

"Then who'd take care of your parents?" She sent him a sunny smile. "Besides, impotence is no defense for murder." She said the *I* word loudly enough for the woman at the next table to hear, to Jack's visible fury. "You'll be sentenced to life imprisonment, and then where will your patients be?"

"What do you care?" he demanded.

"I don't," she retorted. "Your patients have any number of doctors, but Brenda and Dan have only one son."

He sat there, chin jutting out, presumably considering his options.

Then he tossed his plastic spoon down on the table. "Okay, I'll stay. You don't have to ask the judge to order counseling."

She shook her head. "I need every weapon to keep you here. Otherwise you might claim a medical emergency in England and dangle the prospect of a child dying if I don't let you go back."

"As if that would get through to you," he said bitterly.

"I'll lodge the counseling petition tomorrow."

"Just because *you* can't be trusted—"

She held up a hand. "Let's not discuss our trust issues now," she said. "We're going to need something to share with the counselor."

BY LUNCHTIME ON TUESDAY, Callie had employed the full power of the law to ensure Jack couldn't renege on his month in Parkvale.

She'd woken her friend Karen Greene with a take-out coffee and confessed the truth about her secret wedding. Once Karen had got past being offended that Callie hadn't mentioned that she was married to one of Parkvale's most celebrated citizens, her friend was an enormous help.

Karen worked in criminal law rather than family law, but with the experience of her own divorce, she knew exactly what needed doing. By 10:00 a.m., she'd filed an urgent petition that Jack and Callie should be ordered to undergo one month of marriage counseling. When the judge expressed surprise at the petition being lodged ahead of the divorce, Karen confided that Callie suspected her husband would run out on her. The judge granted Karen's request to keep the couple's anonymity, and ordered Callie and Jack to attend counseling once a week for four weeks.

"I'll give you the name of the counselor I used," Karen said when she called in at Fresher Flowers to give Callie the good news. "He was useless, but that won't matter to you." She paused. "Unless you think this marriage has a chance?"

"No!" Callie said, horrified. "This is all about Brenda and Dan."

Karen's mouth took on an unconsciously cynical twist as she eyed a bunch of red roses. "One day you're going to have to start thinking about *you*."

"Believe me, if Brenda and Dan break up, I'll be

as heartbroken as anyone." Callie realized from her friend's frown that it sounded odd. But it was true. She couldn't let Brenda and Dan fall apart, when they embodied her ideal of what family should be.

"This won't stop Jack leaving if he's determined," Karen said. "He could even spend three weeks in Reno and get a divorce there."

"He might just as well be here for a month in that case." Callie tied the last ribbon around the arrangement of tulips and ferns she was working on.

"Hmm." Karen touched a finger to a yellow tulip. "This is pretty. Who's your lawyer?"

"Your sister's stepfather-in-law." Callie slid the arrangement into a vase and set it on a display shelf behind the counter.

"Sam Magill? You're kidding!"

Callie shook her head.

"I'll call him and let him know what's going on." Karen grinned. "He should be used to Parkvale women and their weird weddings by now." She pulled a folder from her tote. "I have two copies of the judge's ruling. Do you want me to deliver one to your husband?"

"No thanks. I want that pleasure all to myself."

CHAPTER FIVE

FOR THE LAST hundred of its hundred and thirty years, the administration offices of Parkvale High School had been housed in the Spanish-style, pink stucco building that fronted High School Road.

Everyone who mattered to her had passed through these doors, Brenda thought as she waited below the arched entry. Dan, Frank and Nancy and their kids, Jenny Gough, as Callie's mom had been then, Jack, Lucy, Callie...

The thought of generations coming and going—from the school, from the town—didn't comfort her the way it usually did. Tonight she could only think of the people who would never come back. Jenny, of course. And often she'd that worried Jack wouldn't, though he was here now. But mainly she thought about Lucy.

Brenda's ankles wobbled in her high heels; she put a hand on the wrought-iron railing, allowed it to take her weight a moment. The timing of tonight's school board meeting was awful—not through anyone's intention—but there was no getting around it.

She glanced at the watch with a mother-of-pearl face Dan had given her for their twenty-fifth anniversary. Five minutes before seven. Clouds had rolled in overhead while she waited, and the air smelled musty, heavy with the promise of rain.

Hurry up, Dan.

A couple of the board members walked by, conferring among themselves. They glanced at her. Were they talking about her? She pressed against the railing, away from them. *Calm down, Brenda. They're not plotting against you.* She didn't know where that absurd suspicion that hit her sometimes came from.

"Brenda." Callie hurried toward her.

Brenda's gloom lifted enough for her to smile. "I didn't expect you, sweetie. Thank you, I need all the support I can get."

"I thought Jack was coming, too?" Callie said.

"That's him now." Brenda pointed to her son, approaching from the south. She squinted... He was alone. *Blast.*

Jack took the stairs two at a time. "Hi, Mom." He kissed her.

"Where's your father?" Brenda asked.

"Still at the store. A couple of builders came in, didn't look like they were in any hurry to leave."

Brenda cursed, nothing too shocking.

"Mom!" Jack stuck his fingers in his ears. She'd never cursed in front of the children, not once. Brenda rolled her eyes, but also blushed.

Overhead, the clock in the tower chimed seven. "We'd better go in," she said.

The six members of the school board sat on the stage at the front of the hall. The president, Alvin Briggs, nodded toward Brenda, but he looked far from enthusiastic.

She headed for the front row. Only half a dozen parents had bothered to turn out, so she had her choice of seats. Jack sat on her left, Callie on the other side of Jack.

Brenda watched the door until Alvin called the meeting to order. Dan wasn't going to make it. Fingers curled under the edge of her seat, she fixed her gaze on the stage.

CALLIE WAITED UNTIL the previous meeting's minutes were being reviewed before she pulled the long white envelope Karen had given her from her purse, and passed it to Jack. "This is for you."

It had seemed sensible to give it to him at the meeting, rather than at Brenda's house, where he might be mad enough to let slip too much information in front of his parents.

He tore open the envelope, unfolded the paper inside. It was identical to the one that remained in Callie's purse—a simple announcement of the court petition and its result.

Jack stared at it for several long seconds. Then he screwed the paper into a ball and dropped it on the floor. Principal Smith, who according to the agenda would present a new antilitter campaign to the board tonight, coughed. Jack looked as if he was considering a one-fingered salute to the honorable gentleman, but he picked up the balled paper and jammed it in his jeans pocket. All without looking at Callie.

On stage, someone voted to ratify the minutes from the last meeting. Someone else seconded the motion.

"I've found a counselor," Callie whispered to Jack,

as the vote passed unanimously. "He can see us on Friday."

"I refuse to attend counseling for a nonexistent marriage," he hissed.

"That piece of paper says you have to, if you want a divorce."

He bared his teeth in a silent snarl. "What the hell are we supposed to say to the guy?"

"Whatever you like. I thought I'd start by telling him you forget my birthday every year."

He huffed. "I don't even know when your birthday is."

"I know yours." She joined in the applause for the baseball coach and his team's outstanding results so far this season. "If you're looking for something to say," she offered, "you can tell him I'm manipulative, and all those other mean things you said about me."

His lips clamped so tight, Callie thought steam might come out his ears.

"Look, Jack, even if we sit there in silence for an hour—"

"An hour!"

"—you'll have met the judge's requirements. You'll have that divorce before you know it."

Callie realized that while they were arguing, the meeting had moved on. She made a shushing motion at Jack, which didn't improve his mood any.

According to the president, the school was proposing to adopt a life-skills training program for freshman students. He read through the curriculum, which ranged from listening, to family relationships, to budgeting.

"Mrs. Brenda Mitchell has applied to address the board on this issue," he said. Last year, the board had voted against the program after Brenda objected.

She got to her feet and headed for the stage.

"Mrs. Mitchell, you have a maximum of five minutes to present your view. Please identify yourself and state your home address and the topic to be addressed."

"For goodness sake, Alvin," Brenda said. "Everyone on this board knows me and knows why I'm here."

"Please also refrain from making vulgar, loud or irrelevant comments." Alvin read the points of meeting etiquette from a piece of paper. "Individuals failing to comply with specified standards of decorum will be asked to vacate the premises forthwith." Elbows on the table, he propped his chin in his hands, as if he expected Brenda to take the full five minutes, and he wasn't looking forward to it.

Jack gave Callie a glance that said *This guy is an ass,* and for once she agreed with him.

Brenda dutifully gave her name and address. "I wish to broach the topic of the life-skills training course. As you all know, my daughter, Lucy, drowned eight years ago during a school picnic."

Sympathetic murmurs rose around the table.

"Lucy's death was an accident. Dan and I never blamed anyone." Brenda's voice shook. "One good thing to come out of that accident—the *only* good thing—was this school's commitment to teaching ninth grade students comprehensive first aid and resuscitation skills."

The initiative had been Brenda's idea, her creation. She'd consulted with experts to figure out the most valuable lessons for the kids, and put together the five-day Lucy's Lifesavers program, a blend of classroom lessons and hands-on activities, with the help of local emergency services personnel.

"We've run Lucy's Lifesavers the past eight years," the principal interjected. Callie couldn't tell whose side he was on.

Brenda nodded. "Last time the board talked about the life-skills program, it was as a replacement for Lucy's Lifesavers. Is that still the case?"

"Our curriculum is crowded enough that we don't have room for two specialty programs," the principal confirmed. "But if we adopt life skills, there would still be opportunities for students to learn first aid."

"The way they used to learn it," Brenda said fiercely. "The old way, which meant that when that courageous boy jumped in to rescue Lucy, and dragged her from the water, no one had more than the most rudimentary knowledge of what to do next." The principal started to speak, but Brenda overrode him. "It wasn't enough to save her," she snapped.

Callie darted a glance at Jack. He sat, arms folded, eyes on Brenda. As his mom's voice grew louder, his brow furrowed. He glanced toward Callie, and she read the question in his eyes: *is this her normal style?*

Callie shook her head. She became aware of the dull patter of rain hitting the windows; the forecasted bad weather had arrived.

One of the other board members spoke up.

"Brenda, the entire community applauds your dedication to this cause, but many parents have asked us to offer broader life-skills training."

"There's no evidence that Lucy's Lifesavers has actually saved any lives," Alvin pointed out.

"The skills they learn stay with them forever," Brenda argued. "They may not save a life while they're in high school, but one day, they'll help someone. Someone else's child or mother or brother or sister."

"Dropping Lucy's Lifesavers won't mean your daughter will be forgotten," the principal said sympathetically. "The school has a permanent reminder in the form of—"

"The garden bench my husband built for the quadrangle." The bitterness in her voice was unmistakable.

Just as Callie got a bad feeling about this, Jack stood. "Excuse me, Mom, and Mr.—uh, Alvin."

Callie heard one of the board members whisper, "He's the brother."

"As a doctor, I'd like to comment about the impact of prompt resuscitation on survival rates."

Alvin glanced at his watch. "It'll have to come out of your mother's five minutes."

Jack directed a questioning glance at Brenda, who nodded.

"Research consistently shows that when effective resuscitation is performed promptly, patients with like injuries have a far greater chance of survival than those where resuscitation techniques were inadequate or delayed."

His tone was impersonal, the content factual, yet

Callie's pushover heart swelled at the sight of Jack taking his mother's side.

When he finished, the president thanked him for his contribution and said, "The essential arguments for and against the life-skills program haven't changed since we last debated it six months ago. I suggest the board now votes on the issue."

Last time, Brenda had won the vote easily. But now…it seemed people thought it was time for a change. Every hand except the principal's went up in favor of switching to the life-skills course. Alvin didn't even need to cast his vote.

"I'm sorry, Brenda," he said.

Brenda stuck her hands on her hips, the aggressive stance at odds with her motherly figure. "You're not sorry, Alvin Briggs, you've been peddling your fancy-pantsy life-skills program for months. Don't think I don't know you've been lobbying the other board members in private."

The president gaped.

"You don't give a tooting damn about our children's safety—"

Callie stared at Brenda. Where was the peaceable, model citizen she knew so well?

"You can take your decree—" Brenda continued, only she added a bleep-worthy word ahead of *decree* "—and stuff it down your shorts."

Alvin picked up his meeting etiquette list, waved it at Brenda. "That was vulgar and loud, and irrelevant. You can leave right now."

"Bite me," Brenda said.

Callie gasped.

Jack sprang to his feet, but somehow managed to make it look leisurely. He walked up onto the stage. "Mom, it's time to go."

Callie discovered a new respect for his soothing-crazy-patients voice. Brenda looked as if she wanted to take some of these board members on, but Jack put an arm around her shoulders and walked her off the stage.

In her car, Callie switched on the wipers to clear the windshield while she used her cell to call Dan at the store. Then she followed Jack and Brenda home. Brenda's car could stay in the school parking lot overnight.

Dan arrived at the house just after they did. He shook rain out of his gray hair as he crossed the threshold.

"Why didn't you come to the meeting?" Far from chastened, Brenda was still hopping mad.

"I got caught up." Dan took her hands. "Honey, are you all right?"

Brenda yanked herself away from him. "No, I'm not all right, which you'd know if you'd turned up. The school board voted against Lucy's Lifesavers, and you didn't do a thing about it."

Dan shrugged out of his rain jacket and hung it on the rack behind the front door. "Honey, we knew this could happen. We've had this conversation." He steered his wife into the living room; Jack and Callie followed.

"It's not a conversation when I tell you what I think and all you do is grunt," Brenda said.

"It's not a conversation when you repeat yourself a dozen times a day, either," Dan growled.

"Mom, Dad…" Jack tried to step between them.

His parents had argued over the years, but never so openly. Callie could almost see him reeling with shock.

Told you so.

Brenda and Dan ignored his interruption, and the argument escalated into a series of "You nevers" and "You always"—a guarantee of sustained hostility. Jack threw Callie a *What now?* look. She felt a twinge of sympathy for him…but only a twinge. Time for Dr. Jack Mitchell, neurological superstar, to get some impromptu experience in his role as Jack Mitchell, son of Dan and Brenda.

"Well, good night, folks," Callie said.

Brenda and Dan didn't hear her, but the flare of alarm in Jack's eyes as she left was extremely satisfying.

CALLIE DROVE TO THE Mitchells' on her way to Fresher Flowers the next morning. She wanted to check on Brenda. And she was curious to see how Jack had fared.

Dan's truck was gone from the driveway, but the Jaguar was there. Callie walked into the kitchen and found Jack talking on the phone. When she waved a greeting, he covered the mouthpiece and said, "Mom went with Dad to pick up her car."

"Okay." She pulled a mug from one of the hooks above the counter. "Why don't you carry on, while I get a coffee."

He frowned, presumably at her temerity in giving him permission to do anything, and turned away to look out the window while he resumed his call. The person on the other end was another doctor, judging by the amount of jargon flying.

Was there any chance Jack was handing in his resignation to his boss, so he could spend more time with his family?

Not likely. He might have got a glimpse last night of how his mom needed him, but he wouldn't see that he needed his family in return. And given that he was essentially selfish, he wasn't likely to make any drastic changes unless they suited his needs.

She wondered if Jack felt any need at all. He had everything—a loving family, a top job, plenty of money...*a great butt*. Callie gave a squeak of embarrassment. The thought had sneaked in, prompted by the view of Jack framed by the sunlight streaming in the window, his fitted jeans emphasizing said butt and a pair of long legs.

He caught the sound and his gaze drifted to her, wandered over her short-sleeved yellow cardigan, her strappy white sundress, and down her legs. Callie assumed he was checking her out on autopilot; he still seemed engrossed in his call. She caught herself running her hands through her hair to fluff it up. Apparently she was on autopilot, too.

She stopped fluffing and busied herself pouring the last of the coffee from the pot on the counter into a mug.

"I don't know, Jeremy." Jack jotted something on a pad. "With a cavernoma you never really know if the surgery got it all. I'd be reluctant to recommend stereotactic radiosurgery without more to go on."

He talked in that vein for another minute, before dropping back into regular English to ask, "Any update on Paris?"

Paris what? A Paris vacation? Paris Hilton?

Jack made a couple of frustratingly noncommittal sounds in response to whatever he was hearing. Then he said, "How's Hannah?"

His voice softened, and he listened intently to the reply. Was Hannah his girlfriend? Maybe she was someone he wanted to date, Callie speculated, but he was waiting until he was divorced. Maybe he wanted to take her to Paris.

"Tell her I'm thinking of her," he said.

When Jack finished his call, Callie asked, "Is Hannah your cat?"

He frowned. "I don't have a cat."

"Of course you don't," she said. "Only people who want to share their lives with others have cats. Is she your girlfriend?"

"Wouldn't a girlfriend fall into same category as a cat?" He cocked an eyebrow lazily.

"I suspect you could ignore a girlfriend, but cats have a way of nagging," she said.

His lips twitched. "You know a lot about nagging?"

"Some." She grinned, and felt the sizzle of attraction. Jack held her eye.

Callie broke away first. She took her coffee out of the microwave. Brenda liked weak filter coffee and Dan preferred budget-brand instant, so drinking coffee in this house usually required gulping it down.

This time, however, a rich aroma met Callie's nostrils, and the liquid in her red Dan's Hardware mug wasn't transparent. It seemed Jack was, in his coffee at least, a man of discriminating good taste. She sipped it. "Mmm."

"That was my coffee," Jack protested.

She raised her mug in salute.

"Why are you still here?" he asked. "I told you, Mom and Dad are out." He'd dodged the question about his girlfriend, she noticed.

"I wanted to see how you got on last night. If you need any moral support."

"*Now* you offer support," he said. "You'll be pleased to hear I handled things just fine. Mom and Dad's little tiff seemed to have blown over this morning."

Little tiff? "You did notice—" Callie set her coffee down on the counter "—that your mother told the president of the school board to stuff his policy down his shorts, and to bite her? Not to mention her expanded vocabulary."

Jack grabbed the mug and took a swig. "Okay, so she got carried away."

Callie folded her arms, stared him down.

"Don't worry, we won't let her do it again," he said.

"*We?* Won't *let* her?" Callie couldn't decide which part of that was more wrong.

She scowled as Jack added sugar to her coffee. He handed her the cup.

"I'm her family and you like interfering," he said. "So I figure, yeah, it's 'we.' I told Mom she needs to accept that Lucy's Lifesavers has been officially voted out."

"It's a wonderful program," Callie said.

"It *was*," he said. "I can't see the board changing its mind."

"I guess not." She frowned into her sweet coffee.

"So for Mom to keep challenging the school on it will only cause more tension at home," Jack said.

"The tension you told me didn't exist?" Callie couldn't resist.

"That's the one."

To her surprise, he didn't seem to begrudge her being right.

"I can understand her being upset about Lifesavers," she said. "What worries me is her extreme reaction."

"That's why I plan to put an end to it."

She tried to drink the coffee, but the sugar put her off. She gave it back to him. "I'm impressed that you're taking this seriously. Even if you're being high-handed about it."

"Thanks. High-handed is a compliment, right?"

She ignored that. "But I think you may be overconfident."

"Overconfident *and* high-handed."

She swatted him. "What if you can't 'put an end to it' before you're due back in England?"

"I can, don't worry."

"But what if you can't?"

He let out an exasperated breath that told her nothing would stop him returning to England. "I've said my piece to Mom, and she took it seriously. I know she trusts your judgment, so you need to give her the message, too. Tell her she can't pursue the Lifesavers program."

"But it means so much to her. I was wondering if we could persuade the school to—"

"No," he said. "We stop this now. Okay?" His imperious tone demanded obedience.

Unfortunately, she knew he was right.

"I feel as if you just offered me thirty pieces of silver and I'm already figuring out to spend them," she grumbled.

"I'll take that as a yes." Jack touched the back of her hand where it rested on the counter. "Work with me here, Callie. Give me something that says you and I can cooperate, for Mom's sake. That we can put aside our differences and get through the next couple of weeks without making things worse."

Her skin burned from the contact; Callie stared at it as if she could see the heat. She slid her hand free.

Brenda needed love and support from Jack, and Jack was making a start. Callie needed to encourage his active interest in his family, not oppose it. "I'll tell her," she said.

Jack smiled. It went all the way to his eyes, which warmed to the color of smoke. "Thanks. You're doing the right thing—*we're* doing the right thing. We'll have peace restored in no time."

His hand covered hers this time.

Butterflies started rioting in Callie's stomach. So much for restoring the peace.

"By the way," she said, "we have our first counseling appointment tonight."

CHAPTER SIX

THE MARRIAGE COUNSELOR worked out of his home in Gleason, ten miles from Parkvale. Jack told his mom he'd asked Callie to show him around the area, and they left in her car right after dinner.

Jack glanced across at Callie. She'd dressed to impress for this appointment, in one of those trademark short skirts of hers, this one white with a pattern of green leaves. With it, she wore a clingy green wrap top, and her sandals had green and yellow rhinestones on the straps. She looked like springtime.

She smelled like springtime, too.

"The divorce papers arrived from Sam today," he told her. "I have them here. You can sign them tonight."

She gave him a small smile and shook her head. Jack tried to feel ticked off, but it didn't work. Maybe because they'd officially joined forces to help Brenda, so technically, Callie was on his side.

They arrived in Gleason and found their destination easily: a newish house, bland and boxy, with a barnaclelike cabin stuck on the front. Jack assumed that was the counseling room or torture chamber or whatever it was called.

Marvin Japes must have cut his counseling teeth during the swinging, free-love seventies. "Groovy to meet you guys," he said.

Where had Callie found him?

The beige vinyl seats were sticky and squeaky, but Jack had no intention of getting comfortable. Marvin's first few questions focused on the basics, such as how long they'd been married, how long they'd been living apart. Which happened to be the same answer, so that was easy.

Marvin scratched his ear as he processed that. "I understand this is court-ordered counseling."

Jack nodded, and shot Callie a dirty look, but it was halfhearted.

They'd agreed they wouldn't tell the counselor any more than he needed to know. Callie had volunteered to manufacture some discussion points. Fine with Jack, if that was her idea of fun. He planned to say nothing at all.

"Perhaps you two can tell me any special topics you'd like to discuss," Marvin said.

If Callie mentioned *impotence*...

"I'd like to talk about my husband's girlfriend," she said.

Throttling was too good for her.

Marvin raised his eyebrows. He made a note on his pad. "Okay, that's groovy. How about you, Jack?"

"Nothing."

That, apparently, wasn't groovy. Marvin frowned. "We'd better start with the girlfriend, then. Who is she, Jack?"

"I don't have a girlfriend," he said firmly.

"Maybe not now, but he did," Callie chirped.

How did she know about Diana? Had Brenda told her, or was it a lucky guess?

"Has that relationship ended, Jack?" Marvin asked.

"Uh-huh." Then Jack decided, what the heck, why not play this Callie's way? "Diana dumped me when she discovered I was married."

Marvin perked up and said a heartfelt, "Groovy." Then he added, "Though I should tell you that infidelity is very damaging to a marriage."

"We're getting divorced," Jack reminded him.

"Uh-huh. So, you told..." Marvin glanced down at his notes "...Diana you were married, and she broke off your relationship. How did that make you feel?"

"Relieved," Jack said. "She wanted me to give her some idea when I'd be ready to live with her, ready to get married and so on. A schedule."

"What a lot of pressure for you," Callie said sympathetically. "She sounds totally unreasonable."

Jack could think of only one woman he'd call totally unreasonable, and it wasn't Diana. "I mentioned that I couldn't think about marriage because I'm already sort of married."

A hiccup of laughter escaped Callie. "How can you be *sort of* married?"

"That was *her* question," he said grimly. "Only she wasn't laughing. She told me I'm either married or I'm not. She didn't want to be with me until I straightened out the situation."

"I like the sound of her," Callie murmured.

"This from a woman who got engaged during our marriage."

Marvin's eyes bugged out.

"Good point." Callie dipped her head in concession. "Is that why you want the divorce? So you can marry Diana?"

Marvin's head swiveled from one to the other.

"She told a friend her troubles," Jack explained. "Within a week, the news was all around the hospital. I was getting so many nudge-nudge, wink-wink comments from my colleagues about what a sly dog I was with my secret schoolgirl bride, it was intolerable."

He was used to inspiring awe and admiration among his peers, not jokes.

"I've progressed through the ranks faster than some people approve of." He addressed Marvin, but the information was for Callie. "I don't want to be in a position where my career could be screwed by someone accusing me of conduct unbecoming a physician."

More than anything, the very real possibility that he might be turned down for the Paris exchange had prompted him to use up some of the vacation days he'd stockpiled, to fly home and get a divorce.

"So, do you want to get back with Diana?" Marvin pressed him.

Jack was having trouble even conjuring her image. It must be because Callie's light, floral scent was so different from Diana's sophisticated fragrance. "She knew I never wanted that level of relationship."

Callie made a zipping gesture across her lips and gave him a virtuous look that said she was nobly refraining from comment.

Marvin glanced from her to Jack. "Guys, I'm picking up on a vibe between you, an attraction thing."

Callie hunched in her vinyl seat, as if to put more distance between herself and Jack. "No way."

"Uh-uh." Jack shook his head.

Marvin wrote something down, then moved on. When he reached the end of his questions, he closed his notebook, "You guys are doing really well."

"That wasn't so bad," Callie said as she and Jack climbed into her Honda.

"It was groovy," he agreed.

She laughed. Her laugh was easy to listen to, open and free. The kind that made a guy want to forget about the pressures, his responsibilities.

"Maybe we should send your parents to Marvin," she said.

"My parents will be fine."

Callie hoped he was right…but she doubted it.

Their silence on the drive back to Parkvale was companionable. When they reached the high school, Callie pulled over.

"What's up?" Jack asked.

"I thought you might like to see the bench your father built in memory of Lucy." She reached for the door handle. "Since it figured in Brenda's speech last night."

For a moment, he didn't move. Then he shrugged. "If you want."

It was eight-fifteen, so the sun hadn't quite set. They walked briskly in the evening chill, heading for the quadrangle behind the admin block.

The cherrywood bench was on the north side,

facing south. Whoever sat there would feel the full glare of the sunshine in the warmer months.

"Here it is, the Lucy Mitchell Memorial Bench," Callie said. "Lucy loved to have the sun on her face."

Jack nodded. He circled the bench, took in the arms carved with a leaf pattern, the slatted seat. "Dad did a nice job."

Callie walked around the back. "There's a plaque here." She read: "In loving memory of Lucy Mitchell."

Jack came to read it, too. He traced the letters engraved into the brass plate with his fingers.

Callie plunked herself down on the bench. After a moment, he did the same. The wooden seat was comfortable, still slightly warm from the sunny day. They sat for several minutes, looking out at the buildings where they'd both gone to high school, years apart.

"Why didn't you want to commit to Diana?" Callie asked.

He shifted next to her. "We're not in counseling now."

"I'm your wife. I'm entitled to know." She spread her fingers on her knees. "Were you too busy? Or just not willing to let someone be that important to you?"

"None of your business."

"It was your impotence, wasn't it?"

He hooked his thumbs in the pockets of his jeans in a posture that shrieked "potent male" and said, "It looks like I'll be offered a two-year surgeon exchange in Paris. Diana didn't want me to take it without making some kind of commitment to her first. I wasn't sure how Paris would pan out, and I didn't want to have to worry about her."

Callie hadn't expected anything like that. Her heart sank. "Paris, Texas?"

He shook his head. "The other one."

How could Parkvale, Tennessee, compete with Paris, France?

"I suppose you really want the Paris gig," she said morosely.

He shrugged, but there was a gleam in his eyes that she might have thought mischievous if she didn't know Dr. Jack Mitchell took himself way too seriously. "I'd have a high six-figure salary, work in one of the most beautiful cities in the world, alongside the best people in the field. Then there's the satisfaction of breaking new ground and saving lives, the great coffee...."

Her heart plummeted further. He wouldn't have a minute for his parents, once Paris got its claws into him.

Not to mention those Frenchwomen. "You'll probably date a French supermodel," she muttered.

"With any luck," he agreed. His expression became calculating and he patted her shoulder. "After you and I are divorced, of course."

His hand stayed on her shoulder another moment, and Callie didn't move away. "What if you marry her, and you end up living in France forever?"

"It could happen." He rubbed his chin. "We'd have great-looking kids."

Callie put a few inches of space between them on the bench. "They get fat," she warned.

He raised a skeptical eyebrow. "Kids?"

"I know they say Frenchwomen don't get fat, but

when you see some of those older women—the ones sitting in the doorways of village shops in movies—they're definitely tubby."

"My mom's tubby," he pointed out, smiling at the word. "It's an age thing, not a race thing."

"My point exactly," Callie said. "Anything you can get in France, you can get in America."

"Like, tubby women?"

"As tubby as you want," she said grandly.

He chuckled…then his eyes dropped to her mouth. "I hear Frenchwomen are incredible kissers."

Callie's lips started to tingle. "Maybe, but I'm sure—" She realized she'd forgotten to breathe, and stopped talking to claim some much-needed oxygen.

"You're sure…?" he prompted, his gaze still stuck on her mouth.

Now the lack of oxygen was making her heart flutter. "American women are every bit…" she slowed as her own gaze was drawn inexorably to his firm lips "…as, uh, incredible."

He shifted toward her, and she could see fine lines at the corners of his mouth that suggested he smiled more often than she thought.

"I just wish I could be certain," he said, doing, Callie thought, a convincing job of sounding worried.

"Take my word for it," she advised him.

With one finger, he tilted her chin. "You forget, I don't trust you."

She had a dozen things to say about how wrong it would be to kiss someone you don't trust, to kiss the person you're divorcing. How wrong it would be to kiss *her*. But every single one of them got dammed up behind a solid, desperate longing to feel his lips on hers.

He touched her mouth with his thumb; her lips quivered against the soft, firm pad. Then, with a growl of vexation, of frustration, he kissed her.

Callie knew a second's paralyzing fear that there was no way she could be *incredible* to a man like him. Then a scorching desire took over, the coaxing of his tongue along the seam of her lips had her opening to him, and she fell into the kiss.

He explored her mouth, seeking, tasting. He grabbed her waist, tugged her along the wooden bench until she was closer to him.

Callie wound her arms around his neck, flattening her curves against him, demanding deeper access to his mouth. He groaned, and the kiss moved to a new level of urgency.

When she pulled away—because if she stayed in his arms any longer she might do something stupid— her hair was standing out in all directions, there was so much static electricity in the air. She put a few inches between them, patted her hair down and rubbed the goose bumps on her arms.

Jack cleared his throat. "What happened there?"

"Maybe the counseling's working already."

He looked alarmed. "It's not supposed to work."

"Karen said Marvin's useless," she admitted.

"So the counseling's not working," Jack said firmly. "Absolutely not."

"Marvin thought we have a vibe," he mused. "I figured he'd been popping some seventies hallucinogens."

"Most likely," she agreed. *Maybe I've been popping them, too.* Because right now, the vibe was so strong she wouldn't be surprised if the sunset turned psychedelic.

"Whatever it was," Jack said, "kissing isn't a good idea. For us."

"Too complicated," she agreed.

He stood. "Time to head home."

Jack took Callie's hand to help her to her feet. Not that she needed help—it was more about touching her again. About the satiny feel of her skin, the light perfume of her nearness.

With reluctance, he relinquished his grip as they walked toward the car. He couldn't remember the last time a casual touch had affected him so strongly. If Callie wasn't so pigheaded about his supposed neglect of his family, if she hadn't tricked him into spending a month here, if she hadn't been *his wife*…he might have wanted to date her.

BRENDA STOPPED HALFWAY down Winn-Dixie's baking aisle and put a hand to her heart to check if it was still beating.

"Mom, are you all right?" Jack asked.

She dropped her hand to her side. "I'm fine, sweetie."

She was here, wasn't she? That was no small feat, when some mornings she could barely force herself to get out of bed. She always worried that this would be the day when she wouldn't make it.

She'd hoped that Jack's return would jolt her out of her blues. But he'd been back a week, and when she woke up this morning she'd still felt as if she was dead in all but the oxygen sense.

"Okay, you wanted sugar?" Jack scanned the shelves.

He'd accepted her reassurance, just like that. Ironic that Jack, a doctor, couldn't see beneath the surface.

"Confectioners' sugar," she said. "And cocoa powder. I want to bake my buttermilk chocolate cake."

Jack smacked his lips appreciatively. "Coming right up."

Or maybe he *wouldn't* see, like his father. Brenda rubbed at her chest, at the ache that wouldn't go away.

"Mom, you'd tell me if there was something wrong with your heart, wouldn't you?" Jack said sharply. He dropped the sugar and the cocoa in the cart.

"There's nothing wrong, Jack." *Beyond the obvious*.

As the checkout girl scanned her purchases, Brenda said to Jack, "Callie called this morning. She asked me to meet her for lunch at twelve-thirty, after she closes up." She checked her watch. Eleven o'clock. On impulse, she added, "I have some time to kill. Sweetie, could we drive down to the river?"

Jack loaded the bags into the cart and pushed it toward the exit. "I don't think that's a good idea."

Of course he didn't; he was his father's son. He hadn't been to the river since Lucy died, Brenda would swear to it.

When they reached the automatic doors, she took his arm. "Please." Her voice cracked on the word. She adored Jack. He was the smartest, handsomest, loveliest boy the world had ever seen. But he never did anything he didn't want to.

Callie had hinted to her that it made him selfish, as if Brenda might be unaware of it. Truth was, she just didn't think this flaw was as important as his good qualities.

"Mom, I don't want to go there," he said.

Although right now, she'd cheerfully have exchanged her brilliant, stubborn son for a good-natured wimp like his cousin Mark.

She trudged behind him to the car. He helped her into the passenger seat, then loaded the purchases into the truck. When he got in, he said, "Why don't we go somewhere else, Mom? It's your birthday soon. How about I take you shopping?"

WHEN JACK WALKED INTO THE Eating Post behind his mother, carrying a load of packages that suggested he'd been demoted from doctor to gorgeous lackey, Callie nearly swallowed her teaspoon.

He'd been in her thoughts—and, disconcertingly, in her dreams—since he'd kissed her last night. But the flesh-and-blood Jack was even more disturbing than her imaginings.

"I'm exhausted," Brenda said as she dropped her purse onto the booth seat. She sounded animated and utterly content, a million miles from the listless woman Callie had heard over the phone this morning.

"Jack wanted to buy me a birthday gift," Brenda continued. "We ran into so many people as we shopped, I'm walked and talked out."

Jack caught Callie's eye and winked. His mom's volubility suggested she was nowhere near talked out.

"I wouldn't say Jack's a natural shopper," Brenda

said, "but when he applies himself to something there's no stopping him."

Callie's gaze met Jack's again. She thought about that kiss, his thorough, expert exploration, and her cheeks heated. She jerked her head away. Among the shopping bags, she caught sight of a familiar, glossy pink bag with black lettering. "Jack went with you to Lady's Lair?" She tried to imagine him with his mom in Parkvale's only lingerie store.

"That's how devoted a son I am," Jack said.

Callie eyed him critically. "You do look pale."

He laughed. "Lingerie was our last stop, so I'm still getting over it. Thankfully, Mom didn't ask for my opinion of her purchase."

"It was a nightgown, very practical, and I certainly didn't want your opinion," Brenda said tartly. "Although Maxine Steen seemed interested in your recommendations on a negligee."

Callie chortled. Maxine had ten years and a hundred pounds on Jack. "I can't believe you got into that conversation."

"Maybe I like looking at plus-size women's lingerie," he said, straight-faced.

"Or maybe he just wanted to make his mom happy." Brenda blew him a kiss. "He's also made a reservation to take the whole family, including you, to dinner on my birthday."

Callie darted a quizzical look at him. He shrugged, spread his hands, palms up, a gesture that said, *Hey, I'm a great guy*.

She wrinkled her nose at him to say, *The jury's still out*.

JACK'S GOOD-SON GLOW faded about two minutes after he got back to his parents' house and started checking his e-mails.

Several colleagues wanted to schedule him to perform surgery on their patients, and his boss wanted an assurance the rumors that had reached his ears about Jack's personal life were unfounded.

Jack cursed. Since he'd arrived back in Parkvale, pretty much nothing had gone the way he'd planned.

His mom was flipping out on the slightest provocation, he was haunting lingerie shops and having counseling for a marriage he'd never believed in, plus feeling obsessed with kissing a woman who was a royal pain in the butt. Not to mention trying to keep the peace between his parents, formerly known as the Happiest Couple in the World.

Things had to change; he needed a new plan. He'd promised his dad he'd visit the hardware store. He could do that right now. Then on Monday, he'd drive up to Memphis, stay with his friend Adam Carmichael and spend the week at Northcross Hospital. He'd come back to Parkvale for his Mom's birthday and for counseling sessions with Marvin, but other than that, he would focus on his work. And he'd stay away from Callie, from the unique distraction she presented. At the end of the month, he'd make a clean getaway.

Jack closed down his laptop, grabbed the keys to the Jag and headed to the hardware store. He hadn't really talked to his father since he'd got back. Dan was a traditionalist who thought men should talk about football, baseball, cars and DIY. The merest hint of anything more personal made him turn up the volume on the TV. If Jack needed to cover any other ground with him, the store was the place to do it.

Dan's Hardware and Timber occupied a corner site. It was easy for builders and home handymen to drive in off Fifth, pick up their supplies, then exit onto Cale Street.

The building was bright blue with yellow window frames—same old color scheme, but newly done. Jack's dad had the place painted every three years. He believed customers wouldn't trust a hardware man who couldn't keep his own house in order.

Jack parked half a block away—under Dan's rules, family never took a parking space a customer might want—and made his way inside.

Dan was talking to someone at the counter, so once Jack had greeted a couple of his father's long-serving staff, he took a look around. The spacious, lofty interior was as pristine as the outside. Ladders of varying heights hung on the left-hand wall above a display of buckets and brushes, and on the right was Power Tool Alley, the most popular section. Jack caught a glimpse of the timber yard through the open sliding door at the back, just below the small mezzanine that housed the office.

A sign hung from the ceiling in the center of the store, promoting Father's Day: Gifts Galore for Dad. Below it, toolboxes, hedge-trimmers and earmuffs were on display.

The smell of paint and wood shavings and some-thing vaguely metallic combined to send Jack back in time. This place had smelled the same when he'd worked here after school and during summer vacations, from third grade until he'd graduated high school.

Dan came over as soon as he'd finished his conversation. "You after a job?"

"Just wanted to see how the old place is doing."

It took no more than that for his dad to start showing Jack the store's new features and product lines.

Jack took the opportunity presented by a range of foot pumps. He picked up one, examined the valve connection. "Callie mentioned you've had problems with your blood pressure."

"Pah, it's nothing."

"You're on medication?" Jack asked.

"Yup."

"Which one?"

Dan grimaced. "Can't remember. Not a long name, but not short, either."

That narrowed the field to about two hundred. "Maybe I could talk to your doctor," Jack said. "Just to be sure he's on top of it."

His father straightened a stand of car cleaning products. "He's on top of it, don't you worry. Now, tell me, would you use a five-dollar tin of wax on that Jaguar, or would you be willing to pay twenty for the right product?"

In other words, subject closed.

Halfway around the store, Dan's attention was claimed by a woman looking for a tool set for her son's twelfth birthday. The customer always came first, so he excused himself.

Jack observed his father in action. Dan's check

shirt and jeans gave him an air of competence in the same way Jack's white coat did in the hospital. His father was a model of old-fashioned courtesy and respect, grounded in a deep knowledge of his product. No wonder Dan's Hardware and Timber was still going strong in the era of big-box chain stores.

Jack wondered what would happen to the place when Dan retired, which must surely be soon. When Jack was a kid, Dan had assumed his son would take over one day. Jack's full scholarship to Harvard Medical School had been the death knell to that ambition. Dan had taken it well, been immensely if stoically proud of his son, but Jack had felt guilty.

Not for long.

As Callie would say, he'd hotfooted it out of town and hadn't looked back.

His father and the customer settled on a tool set. Dad summoned one of the staff to ring up the sale, then came back to Jack.

"Take a look at these trowels." He indicated a shelf at waist height. "Women love them." Instead of plain steel the trowels and gardening forks were powder-coated in pastel colors and patterns. Jack seized the opening to talk about women.

"How did Mom handle the anniversary this year?" he asked.

Dan didn't need to ask which anniversary. "Same as always."

Jack realized he didn't know what "always" was. "She doesn't seem quite herself," he said. "Are you two getting along okay the rest of the time?"

Dan shoved his hands into his pockets and

thought about telling his son to butt out. It was bad enough that Callie kept trying to dig into his and Brenda's difficulties. But at least Callie was subtle— she respected that a man might want to keep some things private. "You an expert on marriage now, as well as medicine?"

"I'm just asking…" Jack stopped. "Dad, it's obvious everything's not right."

Dan lifted one shoulder. "Your mom always goes funny around this time. Heck, I probably do, too. It's not the best time to be making sense out of our behavior, you know that."

"Yeah."

"It'll blow over," Dan said. Even he thought he sounded more hopeful than convinced.

Thankfully, Jack accepted the answer. He glanced around the store. "I have a couple of hours. Why don't you give me some work to do? I'm free tomorrow, too."

That was more like it! Dan's cuffed Jack's shoulder. "I've got a list a mile long. But I'll start you with something easy, in case you're a little rusty."

"Easy's good."

"Maybe you could do a delivery for me," Dan said. "I'm knee-deep in taking inventory every minute I'm not with a customer. Truck's out back, already loaded."

"Sure. Where am I going? I think I can still remember my Parkvale geography."

"Ingram Street. Down where the railway line used to be." They'd diverted the line around the town fifty years ago.

"I know it. The old rail worker's cottages."

"Number twelve," Dan reached into the breast pocket of his shirt, handed Jack the keys to the truck. "It's Callie's place."

Jack closed his eyes.

"You all right, Son?"

He opened them again. "I'm fine," he muttered. "I should have guessed. In this town, all roads lead to Callie."

CHAPTER SEVEN

CALLIE'S HOME WAS the last in the line of railway cottages. Most of them had been renovated to chocolate box cuteness. Picket fences abounded, and almost to a house, climbing roses spilled over the gates.

Jack pulled into the driveway of number twelve...and cringed. There was nothing cute about this dump. Paint that might once have been cream was now a mottled brown, and peeled from the old boards. The bottom half of one of the sash windows had been boarded up, and a couple of planks were visibly lifting from the front porch.

Only the garden more than held its own. No roses here, just a profusion of flowers Jack couldn't name.

He could see a pile of timber out the back, so he heaved a load of the one-by-fours off the truck and, balancing them on his shoulder, headed in that direction.

The back door opened the moment the new stock clattered on top of the existing wood.

"Hey, come on in for a drink."

The pleasure in Callie's voice startled Jack, tightened his belly, made him think about that kiss they'd shared, about doing it again.

He straightened, sloughed off the thought. Callie stood on the doorstep. Behind her, the bottom pane in the door was cracked from top to bottom.

She wore short denim cutoffs that showcased her legs, and a black tank top that left her shoulders almost bare.

"Oh," she said "it's you." The warmth disappeared.

He gave her a mock salute. "From brain surgeon to delivery guy in one easy step. Did you just invite me in?"

"Uh…"

"I'll get the next load of wood," he said, "while you figure out exactly what you're offering by way of hospitality. But I'm warning you, I'm thirsty."

When he'd finished transferring the timber and several cans of paint, refusing Callie's offer of help, she said, "Would you like a coffee or a soda?"

Which was quite possibly the nicest thing she'd said since he arrived in Parkvale.

"Coffee would be great." As he followed her inside, he ran a hand around the back of his shoulders to ease muscles no longer accustomed to physical labor.

"French press or espresso?" Callie indicated a coffee machine that was the only fancy thing in the shabby kitchen.

He liked a woman who had her priorities straight.

"French press." He'd drunk a take-out espresso on his way to the hardware store.

Callie put the kettle on the stove and filled the press with hot water to warm it, another touch Jack appreciated. Coffee should be served very hot.

She reached high for cups, and her shorts molded

to the lift of her derriere. Jack didn't permit himself more than a moment of checking her out. Instead, he inspected the more mundane aspects of his surroundings. The wooden cabinetry looked to be original, but was freshly painted, though the center island was a newer, prefabricated piece with a temporary plywood top. Turquoise linoleum, streaked with age, covered the floor, and the walls bore traces of decades of cooking in a pre-extractor fan era.

"This place is not a dump," Callie said sharply.

Jack realized she was watching him. "Did I say that?"

She folded her arms beneath her breasts. "You're looking around as if you wish you'd brought a wrecking ball."

He smiled. "Not my area of expertise." He glanced at the cracked plaster ceiling. A large water mark suggested there'd been a leak at some stage. "But, yeah, there might be a case for a mercy killing."

She poured coffee beans—Kenyan, Jack noticed—into a grinder, and for several noisy seconds there was no point in talking. She tipped the grounds into the press.

"Did you think about enhancing your street appeal by painting the outside?" he asked.

She sent him a withering look. "We've had so much rain through the spring, it hasn't been possible. I've started on the inside while I wait for a fine stretch."

Callie tried not to take offense at Jack's tone. He'd only seen the kitchen, the worst room in the house. It was the most expensive to fix up, so she was leaving it until her funds were healthier. But she'd stripped the window frames back to bare wood, which she'd sealed and polished. With the gold gleam of the wood and the morning sun streaming in, she knew how appealing the finished room would be.

Jack obviously didn't share the vision, going by the downturn of his mouth. It didn't help that his powerful presence made her kitchen look and feel smaller.

Behind her, the kettle boiled. She poured water into the French press. "Why don't I show you around while we wait for this to brew?"

The cottage only had two bedrooms, but some years back a second bathroom had been installed. Callie wasn't using the smaller one, so at the moment it was jam-packed with fittings she'd bought for both bathrooms.

"The plumber's coming next week to install the new showers and sinks." She whisked Jack past. "Then I can do the tiling and painting." She did as much of the work on the house as she could—Dan had taught her well—but she drew the line at plumbing and anything electrical.

She showed Jack the sunporch that had been enclosed into the house. "The previous owner used this as a sewing room. But I think it'll make a nice office."

"I like this color." Jack tapped the wall in the hallway, which she'd painted last week.

She grinned. "It's called cappuccino."

She showed him the guest bedroom, a square, featureless space that he carefully didn't comment on. Which meant, for the sake of her pride, she would have to show him her own room.

She pushed open the door, stepped inside and let the room do the talking.

"Wow," Jack said.

In keeping with the cottage's age and simplicity, she'd painted the walls burnt-ochre, which made the space feel intimate and warm, and hung heavy linen cream curtains at the windows. She'd used a generous amount of fabric so the curtains billowed behind their tiebacks. The same fabric swathed the ceiling above her bed, creating an exotic, romantic ambience.

Unlike the rest of the house, which would ultimately have polished wooden floors, she'd carpeted the bedroom, a deep wheat-colored pile.

"The whole house will look like this in the end," Callie said. She pointed upward. "The high ceilings and the original features like the plaster moldings make it worth restoring."

Jack nodded. If his agreement wasn't emphatic, he at least no longer looked as if he was about to have her declared homeless.

Still looking up at the ceiling, he walked farther into the room. When his knees bumped the bed, he stopped, glanced down at her cream duvet and the pile of pillows.

Suddenly uncomfortable to have him anywhere near her bed, Callie said, "On with the tour." She left the room, forcing him to follow.

"What's this?" Jack asked. The door in the hallway had a chair wedged under the handle.

"The basement." Callie shivered. "I have a rat problem." She grinned. "And I don't mean you."

"Very funny." Jack tested out the chair, which she

knew was solidly in place. "Those rats must be pretty big if you think they can reach the door handle." He tried it and found it locked. "Smart, too."

"Believe me, when you're lying awake at night listening to rats scrabbling around, it's a small leap of the imagination to picture them breaking out of the basement." Callie led him into the living room, which later would get all the afternoon sun. She brought his attention to the elaborate cornices that made the room far grander than the rest of the cottage.

But Jack was still back with the rats. "Have you set poison?"

"Of course. But like you said, they're smart. And I'm not keen to go down there and urge them to eat the stuff."

He frowned.

"Our coffee will be ready," Callie said.

JACK ADDED TWO SPOONFULS of sugar, no cream, to the mug Callie pushed across the plywood counter.

"Now that you've seen it all," she said, "what do you think?"

I think it's a rat-infested hovel. I think you're crazy. "It's a big job," he said, with a diplomacy catered especially to her.

"Bigger than I've done before," she admitted. "The other renovations I've done have been more cosmetic. This one's taking longer—and costing more—than I expected. It'll be harder to make a profit." She sampled her coffee and smacked her lips. "But I fell in love with the place—I'm trying to figure out a way that I can keep it." She gazed around the room, evidently seeing admirable qualities that were invisible to Jack.

"I don't see how you can finish this place in a reasonable time frame, when you're working full-time at the shop," he said.

"I'll do it."

"That living room has a lot of rotten floorboards."

"That's what the one-by-fours you brought are for."

"Have you done a floor before?"

"I'm very handy," she said. "Ask your dad."

Jack took a sip of his coffee, let the smooth, rich liquid slide down his throat. For a few seconds, the place didn't look so bad. "You make great coffee."

Her eyes met his over the rim of her cup, then slid away again. But it was too late, he'd already felt that connection, and he could tell she had, too. "Thanks," she said lightly.

"*Can* you afford to keep this place?" He assumed her finances relied on her selling it at a profit.

"Sure, if I don't eat for a year," she said. "And if business picks up at Fresher Flowers."

"You could probably sell a lot more flowers if you didn't talk people into going shopping with their mothers instead of buying bouquets," he advised her.

"But then I wouldn't be able to sleep at night."

It dawned on Jack that he had the answer to the question he'd come home to ask. Was Callie financially secure?

Hell, no.

She had a mortgage to repay. Her business was struggling. She lived in a cottage—too good a word for it—that she couldn't afford to improve at a decent profit. And if she ever managed to fix it up, she'd sell it, rendering herself immediately homeless, and be forced to start the whole cycle again.

"A renovation is a big commitment," he sympathized. "It must put pressure on you when you're trying to make a success of the shop."

"I guess."

"How about we sell this place, buy you a nice condo," Jack suggested. "One without rats."

She's blinked. "There's no *we* here, Jack."

"I could lend you more money."

"Are you trying to bribe me to sign those divorce papers?" she demanded.

"Of course not." He paused. "Would it work?"

She rolled her eyes. "I don't want a condo, I want a home. Like this place."

Jack shuddered. "Then maybe you should close Fresher Flowers and go back to a steady income working for someone else."

Callie's cup banged down on the island. "What's going on?"

"I'm thinking about what your mom would want."

Her eyes narrowed. "You're thinking about yourself. You want a divorce, you've stuck a Band-Aid over your parents' problems and now you're trying to fix my financial worries. All so you can leave town and never come back."

"I don't need to solve your problems before I go," he snapped.

But he did. Because somehow this had become about more than getting a divorce. He'd told Callie, told himself, he wanted to make sure she was okay. But he realized he'd set the "okay" bar at a very low level.

At some stage over the past week, the bar had been raised. He didn't just want to leave town, he wanted to leave with a clear conscience.

Damn.

He shoved himself off his bar stool and paced to the other end of the small kitchen. He should never have kissed Callie. One minute she'd been a pain in the butt he couldn't wait to unshackle himself from…the next, she was a responsibility he couldn't ignore.

This was crazy. Since when did a couple of kisses make him feel responsible for a woman?

Since he'd kissed *his wife,* dammit.

If he'd never felt her lips on his, never pressed against her soft curves, he could have walked out of here right now. He'd given her the benefit of his advice, and if she chose to refuse his support, that was fine. Not his problem.

Jack raked a hand through his hair, aware of her smoldering—not in a good way—gaze. "How much capital do you have in this place?"

She frowned at the change of subject. "About twenty percent of the value." She gave him a figure. "Not that it's your business."

"You can't afford to carry on the way you are."

"I'm not going to move into a condo, and I'm not going to close my business."

Jack massaged his temples, thinking. "What if you keep this place for yourself, and I lend you the money for a down payment on another house, one that's a faster renovation? You'd be able to sell it quickly, giving you more cash to get this place into shape."

It wasn't ideal, because she'd still be living in these conditions for a while. But it would provide a faster track to a decent home.

She liked the idea—he saw the flash of longing in her eyes—but she shook her head. "I can barely afford the monthly payments on this place. Cash flow would be a big problem until I sold the new old."

"Let's do the numbers." Jack grabbed a pen and a piece of paper from next to the phone. She'd paid fifty thousand dollars for the cottage—property was cheap in Parkvale—and she would spend another fifteen to twenty on the renovation.

"How much would you need as a down payment on another place?"

"Ten grand, at least." Not exactly chicken feed, but it wouldn't break the bank, either.

"I can lend you that," he said.

Unconsciously, she licked her lips, tempted. "You're trying to sever all ties with me. How will your next girlfriend feel about you subsidizing your ex-wife?"

"A lot happier than she would about me subsidizing my wife." He scanned his numbers. "What's your net monthly income at Fresher Flowers?"

When she told him, he winced. At his request, she supplied her monthly personal budget. "That doesn't include many luxuries," she said.

"Can you build the business up to a level where you can pay two mortgages?"

"I'd need to put a lot more time into it," she said.

"But if I have two houses to renovate, that can't happen." Her face fell. "It was a good thought, Jack, but it can't work."

She was right, she couldn't do it. If Jack wanted to get out of here without forever worrying about Callie being eaten by rats, there was only one thing he could do.

CHAPTER EIGHT

JACK FORCED OUT THE words that would condemn him to weeks of immersion in his parents' lives, to day after day of Callie's proximity, and most likely endless hours of harassment. "I'll spend the next three weeks fixing up this place."

She laughed. "In my dreams."

"If I can finish the big jobs, it'll at least be habitable," he said. "With this place finished, you'll be able to renovate a new property faster, as well as put more time into the shop."

She was looking at him as if he'd lost his mind. "Jack, what are you talking about?"

"I'll paint the exterior, do the porch and the floors, finish the bathrooms." He ticked off the tasks on his fingers. "And kill the rats."

"You're a doctor."

He frowned. "I learned from the best—I was roped in to help when Dad added the den to the house years ago. The toolbox he gave me for my eighteenth birthday is still in his garage."

She chewed her lower lip, a picture of doubt, realizing he was serious, but not sure how and why he would do this.

A memory came to him, of a spring break back in Parkvale. "You used to think I could do anything. Remember that time you and Lucy rode your bikes into a ditch, and I straightened them out?"

"That's not tiling a bathroom."

"My point is, you used to have a kid-sister hero-worship thing for me. Why can't you find some of that faith now?" He felt a pang of longing for Lucy, who had also worshipped him, while still being fully aware of his faults and unafraid to point them out. Callie had that same ability to point out his faults, but she was sadly lacking in the worship department.

"I'm no longer a kid and I was never your sister," she said flatly.

Yeah, and didn't he know it. He dragged his gaze away from her mouth.

"I won't let you do it. I don't want you working on my house, when you could be with your parents," she said.

"I don't want to work on it, either," he said. "But you refuse to see sense about this dump, so I don't have a choice."

"I can do it myself," she said obstinately. "We'll figure out another way to make it work."

Jack poured himself another coffee—he needed a caffeine injection—then one for her. "Don't worry about me depriving Mom and Dad. If I'm not at your place, I'll be spending the week in Memphis." He told her about the hospital.

"You'd leave town while you're home to visit your parents?"

"It's not leaving my parents, it's going to help other

physicians treat their patients." Why was he wasting his breath? She'd never get the big picture. "I don't want to work here," he said, "but I'm going to do it. You can't change my mind. I won't get in your way, I'll be here when you're at the shop. Just me and the rats."

He watched as she thought it through, her foot tapping on the linoleum floor with frustration.

"Fine," she conceded at last. "You can help."

The words sealed his fate. "Your gratitude is touching."

DAN PARKED THE RANGER under the shade of a sycamore tree. There were no other cars around, but Brenda was here, he knew it.

Not through some romantic sixth sense. The first time he'd arrived home from the store at six o'clock and found no wife, no meal cooking, no heating on, he'd called Callie, and then the sheriff.

Brenda had been mortified when she arrived home a couple of hours later, but not so mortified that she hadn't done her disappearing act again. At least the next time, he knew she'd come here, to the river.

Recently, the trips had become a weekly occurrence.

The track down to the river was clearly marked through the long grass, trampled by thousands of feet. In summer, it would be even clearer, the grass would dry out and brown where it got worn down.

Dan jingled a couple of coins in his pockets as he walked. He was damned if he knew what he was going to say to her. *Snap out of it* was what came to mind. But Callie had told him to go easy on his wife.

He rounded the last bend in the path, between two enormous oak trees, and found himself in the clearing near what everyone around here called The Rocks. The unusual-shaped stones that slowed the flow of the river at this point made it an excellent swimming hole.

Sure enough, there was Brenda, sitting on the grass at the edge of the water, probably getting her fanny damp. She looked up as he approached; he realized he was still jingling those coins.

"Dan!" Her face lit up, and he felt the familiar surge of love that had bound him to her for better or for worse from the first day they'd met in high school. Then he saw the tissue in her hand, the puffiness of her eyes, and his love yielded to the slow-burning anger that had been kindled in him this same time last year. He couldn't seem to extinguish that anger, no matter how hard he smothered it.

"Thought I'd find you here," he said.

"The river's so pretty in the spring."

They both knew she wasn't here to admire the scenery.

"I didn't see your car," Dan said.

Brenda glanced around, trying to come up with an explanation that would appease him, he knew. She blushed, and Dan remembered her cheeks firing up at the slightest compliment when they were teenagers. "I, uh, walked."

"It's five miles," he said, as if he hadn't told her that before.

"It's a nice day. I lost track of time."

"It's nearly dark," he said. "How were you planning

to see your way home? Do you have a flashlight, or your cell phone?"

She shook her head.

Dan rubbed his hands over his face. *Go easy.* He sat on the ground next to her. Sure enough, dampness started seeping through his jeans right away.

"Brenda, you've got to—" *snap out of it* "—stop these walks. I'm worried about you."

"It's a difficult time for me, Dan. I'm keeping everything together most days. You shouldn't begrudge me some time out."

She was right. Most days she was her usual self. But the periods she wasn't were coming more often. "Was yelling at Alvin Briggs keeping it together?" he asked.

Her eyes flashed. "He canceled Lucy's Lifesavers."

"Was crying your eyes out when Sarah tried on her wedding dress keeping it together?" He hadn't confronted her about that before. He'd wanted to think it was a one-off.

Brenda swallowed. "That was bad timing, Sarah setting her wedding date so soon after Lucy's anniversary. No wonder I can't help thinking that I'll never see Lucy get married, or have babies." She added belligerently, "Anyone would cry about that."

"Other people can't schedule their lives around your grief."

Dan saw the moment she realized what he'd said: she gasped, putting a hand to her chest as if he'd stabbed her.

He pushed on, before she could shut him out. "Brenda, do you think you need to…see someone?"

"I—no." She plucked several blades of grass, shredded them with her fingers. "I saw someone back when it happened."

"Maybe he wasn't any good. I never liked him."

"Marvin was fine," she said. "*He's* not the problem."

The words were loaded with meaning. Dan ignored that. He wasn't the one acting crazier every day. He took her hands in his, turned them over so he could see her palms. These hands had loved him, soothed him, cared for their children, made their house a home.

"I love you, Brenda," he said.

She choked back a sob, and for a moment he thought she was going to cry uncontrollably again.

Instead, she drew in a shaky breath. "I love you, too." She curled her fingers around his. "But, Dan, right now, there's so much pain inside me, I don't know where it's coming from. Nothing feels right. It's something you and I need to fix together." She squeezed her eyes closed.

Just like that, he was floundering again. What the heck was a man supposed to say to that? How could she say she loved him, then say nothing felt right?

Dan gazed around the clearing, seeking answers. Nothing struck him, beyond the fact that his butt was now freezing cold as well as wet.

That was it!

"I'll build a bench," he said.

Brenda opened her eyes. "Excuse me?"

"A bench for Lucy, like the one at the school." He released Brenda's hands, clambered to his feet too fast for his stiff back—he heard the crack of vertebrae adjusting their position. He walked a few feet, until he had a good view of the path and the river. "We'll put it right here." He outlined the shape with his hands. "When the kids come down here, they'll have some-where dry to sit. We'll put a plaque on it, like the other one. It can say whatever you want."

He beamed at her, relieved beyond measure that he'd thought of something that would make her happy. Something for Lucy.

"A bench," she said.

He nodded.

Brenda stood up, much more gracefully than he had, even though she was plumper than he was. She walked away, toward the track.

"What do you think?" he called, uncertain now.

"I think—" she looked over her shoulder, swiping briskly at the damp patch on her skirt "—I'm going to walk home. Don't wait up."

IT WAS UNNERVING to arrive home from the shop to find Jack inside her house.

Callie heard a machine of some kind running in the living room. She dropped her groceries on the counter, along with some purple hydrangeas that were too far past their prime to sell in the shop. Then she slipped off her shoes and went to check on her new builder.

She stopped in the living room doorway, staring. Jack must have worked nonstop all day. He'd already replaced the rotting boards, and was using a rotary sander to prepare the floor for staining. He had his back to her, and his shirt off. Dust floated in the air, spark-ling in the early evening sunlight so that Jack looked hazy, a mirage of maledom in the desert of Callie's love life.

"Hi," she said. He didn't hear her over the machine, so she walked across the floor, grit sticking to the soles of her bare feet. She tapped Jack on the shoulder.

He spun around, cursing.

"Sorry!" she shouted.

He switched off the machine, muttering something about heart attacks.

"I can't believe you did so much in one day." Callie gestured to the bare boards.

"Told you I was good." He folded his arms, surveying the room, and nodded with satisfaction.

"Do you want a beer? You look hot." *In more ways than one*. Her thought hovered like the dust. She almost imagined Jack could see it.

He ran his gaze over her leisurely, starting at her shoulders, bared by her off-the-shoulder T-shirt, and touching on her waist, her hips, her legs. "I could do with cooling down," he said.

Callie fled the room. In the kitchen she popped the tops off two Coors and ran one of the chilled bottles across her forehead. She started slicing tomatoes for a salad for her dinner.

A couple of minutes later, Jack joined her. Thankfully, he'd put on his T-shirt, though the way it molded to his shoulders and chest wasn't great for her equanimity.

"I didn't expect you to work so late," she said.

"The later I leave, the quicker I get the job done."

He sat on a bar stool at the island and chugged half the beer in one long swallow. Which meant he should be out of here in two minutes. Callie relaxed as she pulled a lettuce out of the fridge.

"Ugh, lettuce for dinner."

"You're not invited," she said.

"Good." He raised his beer in a salute and took another slug.

Callie watched the movement of his strong, tanned throat.

He caught her looking. "Can I help you?" he asked, amused.

She started shredding lettuce. "So," she said chattily, "you obviously didn't forget a thing your dad taught you. If they ever fire you from that hospital, you can come back here and run the store."

He looked down his nose at her. "They'll never fire me."

She perched on a stool, which made her taller. "Okay, if your head gets so big you can't get in the door, you can come back here."

He chuckled. "Thanks, but no thanks. I never wanted to run the store, even before I wanted to be a doctor."

"What did you want to do?" She couldn't imagine him being anything other than a neurosurgeon.

"Train engineer," he said. "Until I was eleven, I was convinced that was my calling."

"Understandable," she said. "Everyone knows engineers get more girls than doctors."

He laughed and took another swig of beer. He wiped his mouth with the back of his hand, which made Callie look at his lips. *Look away, look away.* Eventually, she managed it.

"Of course," she said, "it's pretty hard to become a world famous train engineer. Or hardware store owner."

He tapped the base of his bottle on the counter as he set it down. "I'm not in neurosurgery for the fame."

"Uh-huh."

"But I did have to think big," he said. "My being a doctor wasn't in my parents' frame of reference. I set my sights on Harvard when I was twelve, but I knew I wouldn't get there unless I saw the world extending far beyond Parkvale." His gray eyes challenged her, but he said lightly, "And now you're trying to convince me to tie myself back to the place."

"I'm not suggesting you have to live here," she said.

"Getting where I am has taken focus. I'll admit that's been to the detriment of my family life."

Which, Callie thought, was a major admission. Could she be making progress?

"But I'm still a long way from the peak of my career," he said, as if warning her not to think that. "I want to be there for my parents when they get older, but right now, I don't want to risk losing that focus."

It sounded so reasonable. Callie sipped her beer, thought about what he'd said. "People die," she said quietly.

"What?"

She pushed the bottle away. "You can't put off your family on the grounds that other things take priority right now. What if you never get to be there for them because one of them dies? Or both of them?"

He shook his head. "If this is about Dad's blood pressure—"

"You may be a genius, but you're not God." Tension tightened her voice. "You don't know what the future holds."

His expression softened. "This is about your mother."

The breath leaked out of her. "You can't *know*, Jack."

He lifted a hand to her flushed cheek. She couldn't draw back.

Jack ran his thumb across her cheekbone, down to her lips. "I think it's sweet that you're so concerned about my family."

She jerked her head aside. "Don't mock me."

His laugh was low and soft. "I wouldn't dare." He was looking at her mouth now, the way he had before he kissed her.

"And don't even think about trying to, uh, distract me," she said.

He chuckled. "You think I could distract you, when you're on a roll about my family?"

"Probably not," she lied.

He took her hand, interlaced her fingers with his. "Let's find out."

Callie had another argument on the tip of her tongue about why he should spend more time with his parents, but now it was wrapped up in a dense shroud of cotton wool, while her mind focused on the sensation of his strong fingers entwined with hers. Joined.

Jack leaned in, bent his head. This time he was gentle, questing. He tasted her lips, her tongue, the sweet warmth of her inner cheeks. Callie responded with growing fervor. Something deep inside her ached to discover more of him.

She burrowed her fingers into his dark hair, and Jack growled with pleasure. He slid off his stool so he could move closer to her. His hands settled at her waist; his thumbs traced the indentation. Nerve endings tingled all over Callie's body. She shivered and leaned into him. One strong hand swept up over her curves, cupping, molding. In retaliation, she slipped her hands beneath his T-shirt and found warm, firm flesh.

He groaned against her neck, tickling her sensitized skin. If Callie didn't stop this now, she never would. She put her hands over his, which only increased the delicious pressure. She let herself enjoy it for two more seconds…make that five more seconds… When she reached ten, she sighed and firmly moved his hands away.

"Okay," she said breathlessly. "That's enough of that."

"You clearly have no idea of the meaning of the word *enough*." He reached for her again, but she sidestepped.

"I'm serious Jack."

"But if we both want to…"

"I don't," she said. He snorted, and she said, "Okay, I did, but only because you said I was right about you neglecting your family."

"Did I?" He sounded shocked.

"You implied it, and an admission of guilt is a very attractive thing in a man. But only momentarily."

"I've done lots of bad things. We can have lots of moments."

Before she could tell him not to be preposterous—

or, worse, urge him to confess all—his cell phone rang.

Jack fished out his phone, looked at the display and immediately took the call. "Jeremy, what's up?" He switched into professional mode; Callie remembered Jeremy was the colleague she'd heard him talking to before.

Jack listened for a minute, then asked a couple of questions. "Much as I appreciate your high regard," he said, "I'm certain Daniel Lee can perform the procedure to the same standard."

Jack Mitchell was admitting someone else was as good as he was?

He dropped into a technical commentary that Callie couldn't begin to follow. She pottered around the kitchen, tidying.

"I'd love to talk to her." The sudden lift in Jack's voice caught her attention.

"Hannah, how are you?"

Hannah, the woman he'd asked after last time.

Callie listened in shamelessly—she figured she was entitled after that kiss—as Jack chatted to Hannah about his "vacation" in the U.S.A. Then she realized he was talking to a child. He teasingly asked the girl questions about her medical condition, then quietly—confidently—calmed her down when she seemed to be worried.

Hannah was a lucky girl to have Jack as her doctor, Callie thought.

"Great to talk to you," he said at last. Then, "You bet I will. Hang up now, sweetie, and tell Dr. Jeremy I said goodbye."

He ended the call, but didn't immediately put away his phone.

"Hannah's a patient of yours?" Callie asked.

He nodded. "She has arteriovenous malformations—a vascular malformation in the brain."

"It sounds serious. Will she be okay?"

"If we can get the lesion down to a size where we can remove it." Jack drained his beer. "I'll do a couple more hours in the living room—just ignore me."

Ha, ha, very funny. Callie's nerve endings would be on tenterhooks the second his T-shirt came off. Or before.

In the doorway, he turned back. "Callie, I have a lot of patients like Hannah. When my month here is up, I'm heading back there as fast as I can."

CHAPTER NINE

DOWNTOWN PARKVALE WAS positively humming on Tuesday morning. Jack had to park two hundred yards from Callie's shop, and fight his way through the crowd—two moms hogging the sidewalk with their baby strollers—to get to Fresher Flowers.

The proprietor of Brunello, the new Italian restaurant where Jack had reserved a table for his mom's birthday dinner, was sweeping his outdoor dining area; he called a greeting as Jack passed. Next to Brunello was R.H. Designs. The sign above the window proclaimed simply Hand Crafted Furniture, but the store was unlike any other in town, or any within a hundred mile radius, Jack would bet. He stopped to admire the simple, masterfully designed tables and chairs and cabinets through the window. They looked comfortable, functional, yet had the kind of detailing that spoke of a craftsman who loved his work.

The positive impression created by the restaurant and the furniture store was wiped out by the next two businesses—a dollar store displaying bins of merchandise better suited to the trash can, and a souvenir shop specializing in Parkvale-themed dish towels.

He managed to get past the souvenir shop without succumbing to the temptation to buy, and stopped outside Fresher Flowers. Unlike the dollar store, Callie's outside displays were classy and attractive. Her logo and the green-and-gray color scheme were as well thought-out as the furniture store's. If her business wasn't thriving, it wasn't because of the look of the place.

As Jack pushed open the door, he remembered the first time he'd come here. When he'd had no idea he was about to encounter Callie, and had been at a loss to explain the florist's assertive mood.

She'd be a lot happier to see him today. By the time he'd said his piece, not only would she sign those divorce papers, but she'd probably insist on kissing him. He might just let her.

From the counter, where she was chatting with a customer, Callie lifted her hand in greeting. She was wearing a short tan dress, buttoned to the waist and belted sexily low on the hips.

Impatient to talk to her, Jack forced himself to wander through the shop checking it out. The impression he'd had his first day back had been of a space that was cool, fragrant and restful—that last quite at odds with its owner's nature.

The same ambience prevailed today. Flowers were banked in vases and tubs; the arrangement looked random, yet Jack concluded it was designed to provide color contrasts and soothing patches of green.

By now, he'd worked his way almost to Callie.

Jack waited. Her customer darted several glances at him, until Callie had no choice but to acknowledge him.

"Rachel, this is Jack Mitchell, Brenda Mitchell's son. He's back in town for a few weeks."

Rachel shook Jack's hand. "You're the doctor, right?"

"That's right." He smiled back at her.

"You're a heart surgeon, aren't you?"

"Neurosurgeon," he said.

She pressed a palm to her breast. "I knew it was something totally impressive."

Callie half snorted, half gagged.

"Not that impressive," Jack said modestly, conscious of Callie's heartfelt agreement.

Rachel put a hand on his arm, and left it there. "You're probably this town's most famous citizen."

Jack doubted that, given she hadn't remembered what kind of doctor he was. But one thing was certain, this woman had a better sense of what he was about than someone else in the room. "It's great to be home," he said. It seemed the right sentiment for the town's most famous citizen.

"If you need any help finding your way around—" the woman laughed at her own obviousness as she batted her eyelashes "—give me a call."

"Thanks."

Rachel looked him up and down again, until Jack felt like the catch of the day. "A neurosurgeon…" she drew a deep breath. "How cool is that?" She giggled.

"Cool, I guess," Jack said. Yet more proof that Parkvale was stuck in an earlier era. A groovier, cooler era.

"Here, take this." Rachel pulled a business card out of her purse. "In case you need some company."

"If I do, I'll be sure and call you," he said.

He sensed Callie's silence turning frosty; it occurred to him that kissing her twice in a couple of days could be considered a sign of interest that meant he shouldn't be lavishing attention on another woman.

He dismissed the thought. It was pretty obvious he and Callie weren't dating. If she wanted to stand around flirting with some other guy in front of him, that would be fine.

He chatted with Rachel, while Callie busied herself with an arrangement of some kind of pink and white flowers, interspersed with long sprays of grass. She did her job well, monitoring her work from all angles, her hands moving swiftly, constantly adjusting.

The phone rang, and she took the call. Jack listened with half an ear. He gathered she was talking to a supplier about some substandard sunflowers.

As he might have predicted, she wasn't about to let the guy off the hook. She was more polite than she was to Jack, but equally implacable in her determination to have the supplier do the right thing.

If he'd heard this conversation *before* they'd started talking about their divorce and his parents, he might have been more wary.

Unlike Jack, the guy on the phone obviously had something to feel guilty about, because he caved in quickly. Callie was gracious in her goodbye, but Jack didn't miss the satisfaction in her tone. Nor did he miss the glance she directed at him, which said, *You're next*.

"Rachel, will you excuse me?" he said. "I need Callie's help choosing some flowers."

The woman took the hint and left. Empty-handed.

"Is chatting up my customers, then driving them away before they buy anything, part of your plan to help me?" Callie said.

"I'll spend a lot more than she would have," he promised.

"New girlfriend?" she asked coolly.

"I can't get one of those until I get a divorce from my nagging wife. The flowers are for Mom. The usual, thanks." When Callie gave him a blank look—because why would she cut him any slack?—he said, "Irises. And something beginning with *D*."

"Not bad," she said grudgingly. "Delphiniums." She moved over to a bucket of purple flowers, pulled out several stems. "These irises don't have much life left in them, so I've marked them down. Maybe I should swap them for gardenias."

"Use the irises. I'll buy Mom flowers again in a couple of days."

Naturally, it would take a lot more than that to impress Callie. Her expression was stony.

"What's your favorite flower?" he asked.

"Why?"

"Just making conversation, the way a husband and wife might."

"Any decent husband would know what flowers his wife likes."

"Humor me," he said.

"Gerberas. And Zantedeschia."

Typical that she'd picked two varieties he'd never heard of. He stared her down, until, with a huff, she gestured to some hot pink flowers with black, licorice allsorts centers. "Gerberas." Next, she pointed at some familiar yellow and green flowers. "Zantedeschia."

"You could have just said lilies."

Her eyes flashed mischief. "Zantedeschia aren't a true lily. It's a common misconception." Her mouth tipped up at the corners, and he wanted to kiss her again.

Not part of the plan.

Jack caught her hand. That wasn't part of the plan, either, but it felt good. "Callie, I've been thinking about what you said about my parents needing me. What you said about people dying. You're right, I can't ignore those possibilities. I've come up with a solution that works for me and for you."

She straightened the sheets of wrapping paper on the counter. "Does it work for your parents?"

"Of course," he said impatiently. "It works long-term and it might even get Mom out of this short-term funk."

"Sounds like a miracle."

"Just common sense." He paused for effect. "Mom and Dad can come and live with me." He amended hastily, "Near me."

Callie's jaw dropped. "In England?"

"I don't mean immediately. But I only need a couple more years overseas, whether it's Oxford or Paris. Then I'll be in a strong position to score a top job back here. Maybe in L.A. or New York, possibly Toronto."

"What will your parents do in New York or wherever?"

"They'll be retired," he said. "They can do whatever they like."

"And you'll see them sometimes?"

He rolled his eyes. "Yes, I'll see them. And chances are I'll get married one day, so my wife can spend time with them, too."

"I always envisaged you marrying another doctor," she said slowly. "Or a Parisian supermodel."

So had Jack—he'd imagined the doctor, at least. "Whatever she does, she'll probably take time off when we have kids. And, by the way, Mom and Dad would be ecstatic to be living near their grandchildren." He shot Callie a superior look.

She crumpled a piece of wrapping paper that was already irretrievably wrinkled, and tossed it in the trash. "You set that megabrain of yours on to the problem of how you're going to be there for your parents, and *this* is the best you can do?" There was no mistaking her reaction: contempt oozed out of every word.

Jack grabbed her by the arm. "What is it with you? I have bent over backward to find a solution that lets me be an active part of Mom and Dad's lives…."

"This 'solution' has nothing to do with me or your parents." She pulled away. "It's all about you."

He flexed his fingers. That urge to throttle her was back. "How do you figure that?" he demanded.

"Brenda and Dan are as much a part of Parkvale as…as the pavement on the roads," she said. "You can't take them away. You can't make high-handed plans for them to move when you decide you're ready to be their son again."

She drew a deep breath and said flatly, "Your parents are in a crisis right now. Not in two years' time. Open your eyes, Jack, and deal with it."

"I can't win," he said, incredulous. "Whatever I come up with, you'll say I'm being selfish." He swung away, then turned back. "What have you ever done that makes you such a great person? Sure, you're here in Parkvale with my parents, but that's because it's what *you* want. My ambition was to be a doctor, yours was to have a home with Mom and Dad. Guess what? We're both living our dream."

"At least I know that family comes first."

"Like your grandparents?" he asked. "The ones who were desperate to have you with them? Once you were safely married you could have kept in contact with them, but you didn't."

He'd thrown her grandparents in to muddy the waters, he didn't expect the guilt he saw in Callie's face. "I wrote them a letter a few years back," she said hesitantly.

Jack was too surprised to take full advantage of having put her on the defensive. He took a step toward her. "Why? What did they say?"

"I'd broken up with Rob, and I…needed some family. My grandfather wrote back." She swallowed. "He told me not to contact them again."

"That's rough," Jack said slowly. "I'm sorry."

Callie had been devastated at the time. Despite her mother's warnings, she'd allowed herself to imagine a happy reunion.

"Mom always said they were unforgiving," she said. "They threw my dad out when he got into trouble as a teenager." Jenny Summers had put the blame for her husband's inadequacies firmly on the parents who'd refused to help him.

"You'd think time and distance might have mellowed them."

"It was a long time ago," Callie said. "I don't think about them anymore."

"Yeah, right."

"Excuse me?"

"Like I said, your ambition was to have a family. Your mom died, you broke up with your fiancé, your grandparents turned you away. You're bitter and jealous," he accused her. "I've got what you want, and that makes you mad."

The words cut the space between them, bled into silence.

Callie's face warmed. "That's a horrible thing to say."

Something that might have been remorse flashed in Jack's eyes, but he clamped his mouth shut and stared her down.

"I—I admit I envy you having two wonderful parents who love each other, and a home that's always been here for you." The words came out breathlessly.

Was that why she was so angry about his lack of interest in his family? Because she was jealous?

No! "Don't try to pass the buck to me," she said. "If you really love Brenda and Dan—"

He held up a hand. "Lady, you are so out of this discussion. Now that I've realized this is all about you—" she wasn't sure if he consciously echoed the accusation she'd leveled at him "—I'm not listening to a damn thing you say."

FOR POLITENESS' SAKE, Callie was trying not to glower at Jack, whom she'd somehow ended up sitting next to at Brenda's birthday dinner. But she was so mad at him that she was failing miserably.

She'd been tempted to not come to the party, but she didn't want to disappoint the older woman. She was glad she hadn't when, as the waiter served their appetizers, Brenda said happily, "This is the best night. All my family around me." She included Callie with a smile.

Callie glanced around the candlelit table. Brenda seemed happy, almost her old self, but Jack was seething. He'd worked on Callie's renovation in complete silence the last few days.

Uncle Frank and Aunt Nancy were pretending they didn't have a daughter about to get married, for fear of upsetting Brenda. Dan was cranky, ostensibly because Jack kept asking if he could talk to Dan's doctor about his blood pressure. Really, Callie suspected, his temper was frayed because the strain between him and Brenda was now so tangible no one could ignore it.

Even by Brenda's undemanding standards, it was a stretch to call this the "best" night.

Callie sipped her wine, a Napa sauvignon blanc Jack had ordered, and which was therefore probably expensive. She found it bitter. Or maybe, as Jack had said, that was just her.

She glared at him sideways and he scowled back.

"Couldn't you think of anything more imaginative to order?" He flicked the edge of her plate.

"I like salad." She eyed his grilled cheese and bacon bruschetta. "And I like my blood to move freely through my arteries." Callie raised her glass. "Here's to you, Brenda, and to happy times ahead."

Glasses clinked around the table.

"I'll have happy times ahead when you divorce me," Jack muttered.

"If you can be happy while you're making your parents *un*happy, more power to you," Callie murmured sweetly.

"That green-eyed monster still on the rampage?"

She clenched her fingers around her steak knife.

"Jack, Callie," Brenda said, "what are you whispering about?"

Callie jerked away from him. "I, uh, was just telling Jack a joke." She forced a smile.

"I love a good joke." Brenda was already chortling in anticipation. "Tell us all."

"Uh, sure." Callie cast around her limited repertoire of jokes. "Uh, Doctor, Doctor—"

Brenda held up both hands. "Mercy! Not one of *those,* sweetie." She laughed. "If there's one thing Jack has no sense of humor about—" there were a lot more than one, Callie thought "—it's Doctor, Doctor jokes. He *hates* them."

"He doesn't hate them," Callie said. She turned to Jack. "Do you?"

He looked as amused as a root canal patient. "I've heard thousands of them, and I've yet to hear one that's funny."

All those years ago, on their wedding day, she'd cracked what had to be the least original Doctor, Doctor joke in the history of the genre, and Jack had laughed loud and long. When, what? All the time he'd hated it?

Callie's cheeks flamed. Had he been laughing at

her? Or just being the patronizing jerk she'd had no idea he was?

Brenda sat expectantly, waiting for a joke.

"I, uh, can't think of another one," Callie mumbled.

Jack was watching her curiously—no wonder, given she was acting like the awkward seventeen-year-old she'd once been. She saw the moment he remembered, made the connection with what he'd said just now. His ensuing guilt made her feel even stupider.

"I've dug up some hilarious jokes for the wedding," Uncle Frank said. "Ouch!"

Callie guessed Nancy had kicked him.

"Mom, Dad," Jack said hastily, "it's time we discussed the future. Yours and mine. Our family's."

Callie gaped. He couldn't still believe his plan was a smart idea, could he?

Jack felt the warning pressure of Callie's thigh against his beneath the table. But since he'd figured out her skewed perspective, the jealousy thing, he wasn't about to pay attention. She had a vested interest in being proved right when it came to his parents. He hadn't planned to say anything to his folks just yet, but it would not only take Brenda's mind off Sarah's wedding, it would give her something to look forward to.

"What do you want to say, Son?" Dan asked.

"I don't want us to be so far apart in the years ahead. I miss you guys."

Brenda drew a sharp breath, pressed her fingers to her lips.

Callie kicked Jack's ankle. He moved his foot away.

"I know I haven't been great about keeping in touch...." He half expected his mom to protest that he'd been fine, but she didn't, which slightly disconcerted him. He stumbled on his next words. "I, uh, my work has been consuming a lot of my life. But you two aren't getting any younger, so although there's no easy way around it, we need to plan on being together."

"Jack," Callie said urgently. "You need—"

He glared at her. "In a minute, Callie. This is important."

His mother's face had broken into a smile that would rival the full moon, and a slow grin lit his dad's eyes.

"I knew it," Brenda squealed. "You're coming home."

What? Jack shuffled back through what he'd said.

"Not *home,* of course," she said, to his relief. For a moment there, he'd panicked.

"But, sweetie—" Brenda sniffed, dabbing a tissue at her nose "—this is wonderful. Where will you be? Memphis? Nashville wouldn't be so bad, either. It's only a few hours." She broke off, grabbed his hands across the table. "Oh, Jack, didn't I say this was the best night?" She glanced triumphantly around the group. "You've given me the best birthday present ever."

Jack gripped her hands, forcing her attention back to him. "Mom…" How the hell was he going to say this? "I didn't make myself clear. I'm not talking about coming back to Tennessee."

Brenda blinked. Dan's voice was husky as he asked, "What *are* you talking about, Son?"

"In another year or two, I'll be done at Oxford." He knew he shouldn't rush this, but he was in a hurry to correct them. "I'm thinking that when I get back to the U.S.A., you can come and live near me."

His words were met with silence.

"You mean, leave Parkvale?" Brenda shook her head, bewildered.

"Not somewhere in Tennessee?" Dan asked.

"No, Dad, more like New York or L.A.," Jack said, all fake heartiness. The names of those great cities appeared to strike no chord of recognition with his parents. "Or Seattle," he said desperately. His folks had wanted to visit Seattle ever since watching that TV program *Frasier*.

"But, sweetie," Brenda said, "this is our home, our history." He knew instantly she meant Lucy. "We can't leave Parkvale," she said. Dan was nodding in agreement.

Jack had come too far to give up now. "Of course you can," he said. "You don't need to go tonight." It was a joke, but no one laughed. "Think about it," he urged them. "My work keeps me a long way away, but I miss you guys." He realized it was true, which came as another shock on top of everything else.

"We can certainly think about it," Brenda finally said.

There was another awkward silence. Dan put his hand over his wife's on the table—his parents looked more united than they had in days—and said, "Thanks for thinking of us, Son."

Callie's words echoed through Jack's head. *"This isn't about your parents...it's all about you."* He glanced at his pesky, smart-ass wife. She was rolling a piece of candle wax between her fingers. He couldn't see her eyes, couldn't see if she was gloating.

He'd bet she was. She'd been right on every count.

Jack couldn't remember a time when he'd screwed up so badly.

CHAPTER TEN

CALLIE'S ALARM WENT OFF at four the next morning. She enjoyed getting up early to travel to the flower auction, but last night's fiasco weighed heavily on her, and she lay in bed, reluctant to move.

A scrabbling sound disturbed her just as she was about to fall back to sleep. She jumped up. Who would have thought she'd be grateful to those rats?

She stuffed her feet into her fluffy slippers, then headed for the bathroom.

And found a man in her hallway.

Callie screamed—then realized it was Jack. She used several choice words to show him she didn't appreciate finding him in her home at this time of night, finishing with, "What the hell are you doing here?"

"Going deaf, thanks to you." His gaze wandered from her face, down her body.

Callie realized she was wearing only a very short cotton nightdress, and the straps had slipped off her shoulders.

"Nice slippers," Jack said, his eyes on her cleavage.

She folded her arms, depriving him of his fun. "You still haven't said why you're here."

"I couldn't sleep after that disastrous dinner, so I thought I might as well get an early start here."

He looked haggard. On Jack, it wasn't a bad look—nothing was—but still, her heart went out to him.

"I'm so sorry about last night," she said.

He knuckled his ears. "I must have misheard. I was expecting 'I told you so.'"

She grinned. "I was getting to that. But you were trying to help your parents in your own thoughtless way—"

"Thanks."

"You couldn't have seen how it would backfire."

"*You* did," he said. "You guessed Mom and Dad would read it wrong. That's what the nudging and the kicking were about."

"It wasn't because I wanted to grope you," she agreed.

Uh-oh, bad choice of words. His eyes were back on her curves.

"Brenda and Dan will get over it," she said briskly. "Cheer up, Jack." She almost preferred him to be his arrogant, know-it-all self.

"You're right, I guess." He sighed. "It's just...I could really do with a hug right now."

Callie didn't hesitate. She wrapped her arms around him, pulled him to her. His chin rested on the top of her head and they stood there for several moments. Callie became aware of his breath against her hair, of his masculine warmth through her thin nightgown.

Of his hands, moving down to cup her bottom.

She sprang back. "Hey! What do you think you're doing?"

"Having a hug." His eyes were wide with innocence, but he couldn't sustain it—he burst out laughing.

"I can't believe I actually felt sorry for you!"

He laughed harder. "If it's any consolation, I feel a lot better."

She huffed, still conscious of the delicious sensation of his hands on her bottom. "You're a sleazeball. I'm going to take a shower, and I'm locking the door."

"Very wise," he said. Then added, "If the reason you're up this early is to cook me breakfast, I can wait."

She snickered. "Flower auction," she said over her shoulder. Aware of his eyes on her bottom, she hurried into the newly tiled bathroom—thanks to Jack—and locked the door. She leaned against it, suddenly breathless.

Jack rapped on the door, startling her. "I'll come with you," he called.

THE DRIVE TO MEMPHIS was nowhere near as stressful as the last one they'd taken together, mainly because the moment Callie hit the interstate, Jack fell asleep.

She decided he found her restful, rather than boring. At least when he was asleep, he couldn't see how often she looked at him. In the regular flares of light from the interstate streetlamps, his shadowed face looked intriguing, mysterious.

They arrived at the auction house on the outskirts of Memphis toward seven o'clock. The auction started at six, but Callie usually contented herself with buying from among the later lots.

She took one last look at Jack, then shook his shoulder.

He rubbed his eyes, stretched until his hand brushed her arm.

Jack let his palm linger on Callie for a few seconds. He felt ratty as hell, but she was warm and morning-fresh, and there were times when a guy needed that.

He followed her into the auction house. The cavernous building had exposed steel rafters and a concrete floor, making it purely functional. But then there were the flowers.

Row after row of steel trolleys held cartons and buckets of blossoms. Jack couldn't have named more than one in ten varieties, there were so many. The heady blend of perfumes permeated every atom of air, the array of colors dazzled.

Callie led him straight through into the auction room, where tiered seating was arranged, with pairs of tables similar to school desks. About half were taken by bidders in varying stages of wakefulness. Jack counted two dozing; several others had their hands wrapped around cups of coffee.

Callie chose a pair of desks right at the top. As they climbed the stairs, Jack saw that each desk had a built-in keyboard.

The auctioneer sat in a corner mezzanine booth. A golf-style electric cart towed a train of three trolleys, loaded with flowers, into the room. Before it stopped moving, the auctioneer launched into a description of the various lots. His assistant stood at the front, using a pointer to highlight each one.

"Are we bidding yet?" Jack whispered.

Callie shook her head, her eyes on the screen at the front that listed all the relevant data about each lot.

The auction ran Dutch-style, starting with a top price, rather than a bottom one. As the clock ticked down, the price dropped. The first bidder to press the buy key would win the bid. The danger of waiting for the price to drop to where you wanted it, Jack realized, was that you might miss out.

Callie didn't take an interest in any of the lots until the third series of trolleys came in behind the electric cart. Jack watched her bid on "Foliage, General" and then on some blue flowers called Gentiana. She was poised to bid for some tulips, too, but lost out to someone with a faster trigger finger.

The excitement over, at least temporarily, Jack glanced around the room.

He tugged the wrist of Callie's long-sleeved T-shirt. "I've seen that guy somewhere before." He pointed out an Asian man in the front row.

"You probably have," she said. "He's a wholesaler who has a couple of clients in Parkvale, including Darling Buds."

"The talented Alice," Jack recalled, to Callie's surprise.

"She's my biggest competition," Callie admitted. "But since I come up here rather than relying on a wholesaler, I can take advantage of any stock that's inspiring."

He nodded. "And you have more interesting combinations than Darling Buds." He quirked an eyebrow. "That's probably not the technical term."

Callie prided herself on her composition, her balance of harmony and contrast in a floral arrangement.

Jack's compliment didn't mean anything. He did not get to say a few nice things and have her eating out of his hand the way Brenda did.

The auctioneer moved on to the lilies. "These will take a few minutes," she told Jack quietly. "If you want to buy a coffee at the cart outside, this is your chance."

"How is it?"

"Better than Brenda's, worse than mine."

"I'll pass."

"Snob," she whispered.

He raised his eyebrows. "I don't see you rushing out to buy one."

She smiled. Jack's eyes traveled over her face.

"Do I have a smudge?" Callie murmured.

"You have every right to," he said.

"Excuse me?"

"You have every right to hold a grudge."

She giggled. "I said *smudge*."

"Oh." That seemed to require him to look hard at her face again. "No smudge. How about the grudge? You were proved comprehensively right last night."

"No grudge," she said, then more mischievously, "How could I, when you provided such fine entertainment?"

She expected him to at least smile—the Jack Mitchell who'd taken himself way too seriously when he first arrived had since proved to have a dry sense of humor that she found way too appealing. But his expression grew serious.

"See, here's the thing," he said. "You weren't laughing at me while I made a mess of Mom and

Dad's future, and you never got around to that 'I told you so.'"

She gurgled a laugh. "Believe me, I thought I'd enjoy seeing you screw up, but I didn't. Beats me why. Though obviously I was never going to be pleased to see your parents upset."

"It all comes back to them."

She nodded.

By seven-thirty, she had everything she needed. She paid her dockets, then Jack helped carry her purchases out to the car. She had a stand built in the back of the Honda that held buckets upright and steady, so as not to damage the flowers on the drive home.

As traffic streamed into the city, they left town. Jack was chattier now, and the trip seemed to pass much faster than usual.

"You won't get to the shop until at least ten," he said when they were halfway home. "Who looks after it when you're at the auction?"

"I have a lady who needs a few hours' work a week. She's not a florist, but she can hold the fort for an hour or so until I get there. And if she's away, Karen's on flexitime in the law firm and she helps out."

"Karen the ball breaker."

Callie tutted. "She's invited us for lunch on Sunday. I hope your manners improve by then."

"Why has she invited *us* for lunch?"

"It's our homework, remember? Marvin said we need to attend a social event as a couple—" the assignment had come out of their second counseling session "—and since there aren't a lot of people who know about our marriage, Karen's offered to entertain us."

"Groovy." he sighed.

She slowed as they drove past a road repair crew. When they were clear, she said, "How will you follow up with your parents after last night?"

"I thought about that all the way up to Memphis." Huh, she'd thought he'd been sleeping.

"I said it all wrong and I got a knee-jerk reaction," he said. "But now that the idea's out there, Mom and Dad will think about it, talk about it." He nodded decisively. "I think they'll come around to the idea. Maybe not while I'm here on this trip, but I wouldn't be surprised if in a year's time they're making noises about moving when the time is right."

Callie held her jaw in place with an immense act of will. "Didn't you learn anything last night?" she demanded.

He bristled. "I learned to be more tactful about how I suggest new ideas to folks who are set in their ways."

Callie banged her forehead on the steering wheel.

"Watch the road," he ordered.

"You're right." She gripped the wheel tighter. "We don't need an accident out here when we have a train wreck going on at home. Let's just hope your parents are still married when they start making those noises about moving."

"They'll still be married," he said. "I think I've figured out Mom's problem. If I can have a talk with her doctor…"

Callie's head jerked around. "What's wrong with her?"

"Watch the road," he said again. "It's entirely natural, nothing to worry about. I'm thinking her

mood swings are menopause-related hormone fluctua-
tions, manifesting as intermittent depression."

Callie laughed.

"That wasn't a joke," he said.

"What would you say if I told you you're suffering
from emotion-related aversion, manifesting as selec-
tive blindness?"

He snorted. "I'd say what the hell does that mean?"

"It means that, as always, you're ignoring what's
going on emotionally. Your mom went through meno-
pause years ago. This is about relationships, not
hormones. You need to think about how you can
change *your* behavior to help her."

"As always, you're jumping to conclusions."

Callie looked at him, perplexed. Somewhere
beneath the designer jeans and the I-know-best
attitude must be something of the Jack who'd let Lucy
twist him around her little finger. The Jack who cared
enough about others' feelings to laugh at Callie's joke
at the wedding, even though he'd hated it.

Maybe she could coax the old Jack to the surface.

"We should go down to the river sometime," she
said. "It's a good place to remember Lucy." Although
his sister had drowned there, she'd also swum like a
fish there most summer days.

Jack scowled. "I'm not going."

Callie tried another tack.

"Doctor, Doctor," she said, "I think I'm a needle."

His eyebrows drew together. "I'm so not doing
this."

She ignored him and delivered the punch line. "I
see your point."

KAREN GREENE HAD ALSO invited her sister Casey, and Casey's husband, Adam Carmichael, for lunch on Sunday.

Callie remembered how Casey used to look after her younger siblings during high school. Back then, she'd always seemed stressed, burdened with responsibilities she couldn't refuse. Now, she was a picture of relaxation and happiness.

And no wonder. She was married to a gorgeous man who plainly adored her.

Casey and Adam had brought their daughter, Lily, and baby son, Trent, with them. Both kids were cutie-pies. One advantage of a great-looking dad. Jack would doubtless produce stunning children, too, Callie thought. With his doctor wife. Or his super-model. She scowled at him. He scowled back.

"Make an effort, you two," Karen ordered. "Or I'll tattle to Marvin."

As threats went, it lacked firepower. But the strain between them did ease when everyone sat at the slatted wooden table on the back porch to eat Karen's paella. Karen's daughter, Rosie, six years old, kept baby Trent amused by pulling faces at him, and she soon had the adults chuckling, too. The Carmichaels were lovely, and it was impossible not to relax into the conversation.

"Do you miss Parkvale?" Callie asked Casey, after the other woman had talked about the joys of being able to work from home. She was an author of novels for teens.

"A little," Casey admitted. "When I left, I was desperate to get away—"

"From me," Karen injected.

"Honey, you know that's not true." But Casey had colored.

"It is, and you were right," Karen said. "I was a pain."

"Anyway, I love coming back to visit now." Casey squeezed her sister's hand.

Jack and Adam were old friends; they'd met at Harvard, where their Tennessee roots had provided common ground. Although they didn't keep in touch much, the conversation flowed easily.

Adam updated Jack and the others about the TV station he and his family owned, Memphis Channel Eight. While other stations were losing out to online media, Channel Eight's advertising revenues were growing at a phenomenal rate.

"Ever thought about taking those superior skills of yours to the big smoke?" Jack asked. "They'd welcome you with open arms in New York or L.A."

"Sure, I've thought about it." Adam caressed Casey's arm absentmindedly. "But Channel Eight is important to the rest of the family. Selling it would cause a riot."

"So you're staying in Memphis for the sake of your family," Callie said. Jack shot her a warning glance. Okay, that wasn't very subtle.

Adam grinned. "It's not the hardship I thought it would be." He dropped a kiss on his wife's lips, and Casey's answering smile radiated love.

She caressed his cheek. "Sweetheart, you'd hate to leave Sam and Eloise."

"How about you?" Adam asked Jack. "Could you move to Memphis?"

He shook his head. "There are a couple of solid

neurosurgery teams there, of course, but they're not involved in the kind of groundbreaking stuff I do."

"These days I think it's who you're with that matters," Adam reflected. "Not where you are."

He kissed his wife again, and although it was brief, the tenderness between the two was almost painful to watch.

Callie looked away, embarrassed by the intensity of the Carmichaels' love.

This was what a real marriage was like.

The comparison to her and Jack couldn't be more shaming. They'd married for selfish reasons, when they barely knew each other. And now that they'd been forced to get to know one another better, their relationship revolved around arguments over his parents, plus their own escalating physical attraction. The fact that Callie liked Jack seemed almost irrelevant.

She *liked* him?

Okay, she liked having him around her house, she'd enjoyed his company on the trip to the flower auction, and talking with him could be as much fun as kissing him.

Minor details, she told herself. Those things couldn't measure up against a true, equal partnership like the Carmichaels'.

She caught Jack's gaze, and looked away. She didn't want to like him, not when there was no chance they would ever end up in a true marriage. She wanted to be in love, to be loved madly in return, to build a strong, loving, close family.

BY THE TIME they left Karen's place, Jack felt as if he'd spent the whole afternoon watching Adam groping his wife. Dammit, Jack's wife was much sexier than Adam's, in his opinion, and he wanted to put his hands all over her, too. Funny how being mad at her didn't affect his desire to touch her.

But touching Callie in that public gathering would have caused a huge stir, considering everyone knew they were in the middle of divorcing.

And yet…there was this undeniable physical attraction.

As they waited at a red light, he glanced sideways at Callie. She seemed pensive, rather than burning up with desire. What would she say if he suggested they took advantage of their limited-time-only married state and got a whole lot more intimate?

A few minutes later, he pulled into her driveway and cut the engine.

Callie twisted to face him. Damn, she was pretty, with her hair curling over her shoulders, giving Jack a glimpse of one ear. In her summery silk dress with the V neck and the enticing slits at the sides, she was slim but curvy. She'd been sexy in a shrunken T-shirt and cutoffs, but now she was irresistible.

He unclipped his seat belt, slipped his hand beneath her hair, found the back of her neck.

"Jack…"

He leaned over, touched his mouth to hers. Mmm, she was sweet, like pralines and pecan pie rolled into one. He coaxed her mouth open.

She pulled away. "Jack," she insisted.

"Uh-huh?" Maybe they should take this inside, he was getting too old for making out in a car.

"I'll sign the divorce papers."

CHAPTER ELEVEN

CALLIE'S WORDS TOOK their time penetrating Jack's brain. What was it about her? With anyone else, he cut right to the heart of any conversation, but with her, his mental processes seemed straitjacketed.

Realization hit, jerking him back into his seat. "What?"

For once, she didn't meet his gaze. "I'll sign the papers now. You can lodge them tomorrow, uncontested."

"Why?" Jack felt strangely hollow, as if something had been sucked out of him. "Why now?"

She twisted her fingers in her lap. "Meeting Adam and Casey, seeing how happy they are, I felt ashamed that we'd got married the way we did."

"We had good reasons," he said. "Besides, the Carmichaels didn't get married because they loved each other." He wasn't sure why he was arguing. *I want a divorce, remember?*

"That was different. Their wedding was an accident. But they're crazy about each other now." She clasped her purse. "It's time to end this thing."

She was right, Jack knew. And she'd just agreed to do exactly what he wanted. He should be punching the air.

He would be, later, he was certain. It was just hard to take in so unexpectedly.

"Thanks," he said. "I guess."

"You're welcome." She was still looking down at her hands.

Jack wished she would hurry up and get out of the car. He needed to wrap his mind around this change in circumstances. But she didn't budge.

"Do you have the papers on you?" she asked.

What was the rush, dammit?

"They're at Mom's place. I'll bring them tomorrow." He put his hands on the steering wheel, stared at the windshield. "

She fidgeted with her purse. "I know this means you might be on the next plane out of here..." She paused, a question in her silence, but he didn't respond. "I guess I'll have to take that risk. At least you've started a dialogue with your parents."

She sounded as if she was trying to justify agreeing to the divorce. He should be helping her, but he couldn't think of a word to say.

"Anyway," she murmured, "it's just not right, what we've been doing, so I'll sign."

Then she was gone, and Jack couldn't remember why he'd wanted her to get out of the car. He drove off slowly, still reeling from the news.

CALLIE WENT TO the Eating Post for Sarah's bridal shower straight from the shop. She didn't expect to see Jack Mitchell among the laughing, raucous crowd. But there he was, propping up the bar, holding his orange juice.

"I'm the designated driver," he said in explanation. "The bride intends to consume several drinks."

"You're here for Brenda," Callie said.

"Are you calling my mother a lush?"

Callie took the cocktail the bartender handed her. "You're worried the wedding will get to her again."

"Dad's worried," he admitted. "He suggested to Mom that he come along, but she bit his head off."

"So you sneaked in with an offer to chauffeur. That's really thoughtful of you, Jack."

"Don't sound so surprised." He leaned closer. "She's watching us, so act like you're not talking about her."

Callie was more likely to act like a befuddled moron than anything else, with Jack so near. It was as if thousands of electrical pulses were trying to jump from her skin to his. She pinned on a bright smile. "How's my house looking after today's work?"

"I painted the living room. I'll do another coat tomorrow. It looks better than I thought that dump could," he said.

She swiped at his shoulder.

"I like your outfit." Jack touched a hand to Callie's hip, and the heat of his fingers penetrated the silky fabric of her turquoise shift dress.

"Careful," she said. "Bridal showers are hives of gossip. It wouldn't take much for people to start thinking you're interested in me."

"Or that you're interested in *me*." He'd obviously noticed that she couldn't seem to take her eyes off his mouth.

"Uh-uh," she said. "They know how I act when I'm attracted to a guy, and this isn't it."

He smirked.

"It's not!"

"Tell me how you act, then," he said. "Just so I don't jump to the wrong conclusion.

"I…" *I'd take every chance to touch him, including swiping at him when he said things to bug me. I'd go weak at the knees just at his smile. I'd see reasons to laugh, even when everything's going wrong. I'd see past his faults to the great guy I know he is inside.* "I, uh…" Callie stared at him. "I'll let you know."

She rushed away from the bar with Jack's laughter chasing her.

She managed to stay away from him the rest of the evening. The shower finished at ten o'clock—this was Parkvale, not New York—and Jack shepherded Brenda and Sarah to the car. "I'll drive you, too," he told Callie.

"No thanks, I have my car."

"You drank three cocktails, that I counted," he said. "Those things pack a mean punch. You're not driving."

Callie counted her drinks backward and realized he was right. "Fine, you can drive me."

"You really do have a problem with gratitude," he murmured near her ear as he held the passenger door open for her.

Callie shivered at the sensation of his breath against her skin.

"You can thank me later," he said.

He drove Sarah home, then Brenda. His mom didn't question the logic of dropping Callie off last, then returning to his parents' house.

"I'll see you inside," he told Callie as he pulled up

outside her cottage. "In your drunken state you're likely to fall through one of those rotten porch boards."

She was ninety percent sober, so she ignored the reference to drunkenness. "That porch is dangerous," she agreed. "The guy who's working on my house is dragging his feet."

His laugh was a huff of breath. He took her by the elbow as they walked up the steps. "I'm thinking I'll make you some coffee, sober you up."

"Mmm, coffee." She unlocked the door, and he pushed it open. "Do you have those divorce papers with you? If so, I can sign them now."

"I have them." His voice was clipped, all banter gone.

Jack left the papers on the kitchen island while he went to wash his hands. Callie scribbled her signature quickly, squinting through half-closed eyes so she wouldn't have to read the words. When she was done, she flipped the papers over and went to make the coffee.

"Let's take our mugs into the living room," she told Jack when he returned. "I want to inspect your handiwork." She also wanted to ask if he'd be on the next flight to London, but she was afraid she wouldn't like the answer.

Callie stepped into the hallway...and saw the basement door ajar. "The rats!" she yelped. "They got out." She looked wildly around, expecting to see rodents running up the walls.

Jack laughed. "Do you really think the rats unlocked the door and pushed the chair away?"

"I told you, they're smart. And strong," she said sheepishly. "Okay, where are they?"

"I got rid of them."

"All of them?"

"There's not a rat in the house," he vowed.

"Present company excepted," she murmured.

He swatted her behind, and she nearly slopped her coffee.

"How did you do it?" she asked.

"You don't want to know."

On reflection, Callie decided he was right. "Well, thanks."

"Gratitude at last," he crowed.

She pulled a face. "I haven't inspected the living room yet—I might revoke my thanks at any moment."

There was no need for that. The living room floorboards gleamed, contrasting with the matte finish on the walls. The color—cappuccino, the same as the hallway—looked even better in the larger space.

As she complimented Jack, Callie was stiflingly aware of him at her side. She'd like to blame the paint fumes for her light-headedness, but the fact was, she'd started feeling like this around him all the time.

She puffed air up over her face as she bent to inspect the baseboards.

"Satisfied?" Jack asked.

The edgy, itching feeling that bugged Callie was the opposite of satisfaction.

"Let me have this." Jack reached for her mug. Her fingers tangled with his, and it seemed to her that he deliberately took his time claiming the cup.

He reached past her to put both mugs on the mantelpiece. His hand brushed her shoulder. Callie's skin prickled, and she dropped her eyes.

"Brenda did well tonight," she said. "No trouble at all."

His gaze was intent. "Nope. No trouble."

"I hate seeing her upset."

"I don't want to talk about my mom," he stated.

"You never do." But right now, neither did she.

"I can think of far more fascinating things," he said. The way he said words like *fascinating,* with a slight British accent, was incredibly sexy.

Before she realized what she was doing, Callie touched a finger to his throat. He sucked in a sharp breath. Her finger stayed where it was, as if the two of them were magnetized.

With his thumb, Jack traced a trail from just below her left ear down to her shoulder. Then lower, to the slope of her breast.

Callie inched backward, then stopped. She didn't want to move away. Jack's fingers seared her skin, and her breath came faster.

His expression was serious, but his eyes were warm with the same heat she knew he would see in hers. "I didn't know, when I married you, that you'd turn out this…"

"Tall?" she suggested.

He chuckled. "I think you're about the same height—" his gaze dropped "—though other parts of you seem to have grown."

Her breath shortened.

"This sexy." He finished his original sentence in a husky murmur.

Callie licked her lips. "I'm still just a small-town girl," she reminded him.

"With a big mouth." His eyes were on her lips.

"Whereas you," she said, more to herself than him, "you not only came back way sexier than you have any right to be—" his eyes lit up at that "—but you're wealthy, educated, a world famous surgeon. You've got the whole package."

"It's a wonder," he said thoughtfully, "you haven't jumped me yet."

She might have known he wouldn't thank her humbly for the compliment. "I figure you're no good in bed."

He released her arm in a sudden movement; his dark eyebrows were a slash of disbelief. "If you're still talking about impotence…"

"It's not that."

He folded his arms, stared her down, dared her to tell his gorgeous, smart, sexy self why he might not be good in bed.

"You don't have to try to impress women," she said simply. "I'll bet they throw themselves at you."

"Not so many that I can't handle them."

"You're right up there without any effort," she continued. "Where's the incentive to improve your game?"

"The reason I don't need to improve my game," he said, "is because I'm at the *top* of my game."

She borrowed the crazy-patient voice. "I'm sure you're right."

To her surprise, he smiled. "So it's your belief that I couldn't, say—" he hooked his thumbs in the pockets of his jeans "—give you the best night of your life?"

Oh, that was unfair! She was practically salivating.

"Not unless I was thinking about your paycheck and your Jaguar." She added virtuously, "But those things aren't important to us small-town girls."

Before she could register the fact, he'd pulled her into his arms. Surely surgeons should move with more care and attention? "You don't need to prove anything to me," she said. "We'll be divorced, and I'll never tell anyone you're impo—"

The rest was lost in the hard, impatient kiss Jack planted on her mouth.

Callie tried to ease out of his grasp, but those long fingers of his were deceptively strong. All her squirming succeeded in doing was moving her tighter into his embrace. She managed to tilt her head back so she could look up at him.

"Jack…" she said reasonably.

"Callie," he said hungrily. Then his lips came down on hers again, and reason fled. His mouth made a lie of her protest, with coaxing, tempting kisses that made her open up to him even though she'd told herself she wouldn't.

When his tongue met hers, he groaned, the sound echoing deep inside Callie. She pressed herself against him, and instinctively his hands moved over her dress to cup her derriere.

Callie managed to extricate her arms so she could wind them around his neck, bringing his muscular chest hard up against her breasts. He explored her mouth with a thoroughness that left her weak, his strength all that sustained her.

"So beautiful," he said into the pulse at the base of her neck. He nipped. "So delicious."

When his hands moved up to caress her abdomen, Callie shuddered with longing.

Shocked at the intensity of her desire for him, she slipped out of his grasp. "Jack," she said, "we shouldn't do this."

"We're married," he said. "We literally have a license to do this."

"We're divorcing. I don't sleep with guys I don't have a relationship with."

He cupped his hands around her face, touched his lips to hers, then pulled back. "Let's just say—" he gave her another kiss "—we're making up—" and another, deeper one "—for lost time." He plundered her mouth again, and she gave up fighting it, gave in, gave herself. Jack's kisses grew more insistent, his hands more exploratory.

"We never got to have a wedding night," he murmured against her ear. He planted a series of kisses along her jawbone. "How about we fix that right now?"

Oh, hell. Did he have to say that?

He began steering her in the direction of her bedroom. Callie regrouped the few brain cells that hadn't gone AWOL, tried to decide whether she should tell him the truth.

Too much of their history was grounded in secrets and deception. She couldn't let Jack make a wrong assumption, even after all these years.

"I did," she blurted.

"You did what, sweetheart?" His hands stroked her thighs as he guided her past the rat-free basement door.

"I had a wedding night," she said.

He stopped in the doorway of her romantic, burnt-ochre room. "What do you mean?"

"The night…after we got married. Um, Rob and I…"

Shock came over his face, so complete that she rushed through the rest. "Rob and I made love. For the first time."

Jack released her with a gentle precision that gave no indication of how she'd sucker punched him.

"You slept with your *boyfriend* on *our* wedding night?" His voice rose, betraying him.

She turned bright red. "Obviously I wasn't going to sleep with a stranger." She took in his clenched fists, his stiff shoulders. "I'm sorry. I didn't mean to upset you."

"I'm not upset!" he roared, so incredibly upset that he didn't like to analyze the fact. "What's it to me if I save you from your evil grandparents, and you go out and sleep with the next guy who comes along?"

"He was my boyfriend," she hissed. "You and Mom came up with the wedding idea and I went with it, but the whole thing was terrifying. I couldn't face what I'd done, and…" She paused, her eyes wide. "I didn't want to feel married to you!"

"Cheating on me would have helped with that," he agreed sarcastically. He would give anything to perform brain surgery on Rob, without an anesthetic.

"You know we weren't married in that way." She took a deliberate step out of the bedroom doorway, into the hall, and carried right on back to the living room.

Jack followed. "I can't believe you went right out and slept with—with *Rob*." Jack couldn't believe how mad he felt about it, either. "You were just a kid."

"Seventeen," she said evenly. "And yes, I was too young. But it was a screwed-up day, and I made a mistake. I did…" She hesitated, then said awkwardly, "I was crazy about Rob. I loved him."

He snorted.

She picked up the coffee she'd abandoned when he'd started kissing her. "You're not trying to tell me you've stayed faithful to me the past eight years, are you?"

"I was twenty-six," he said. "And I didn't sleep with someone the day we got married." He knew it was totally unreasonable to suggest that his waiting a few weeks or months to sleep with someone made him any kind of saint. And, yeah, he was being a chauvinist and a jerk. But…

"I came looking for you," he said abruptly, remembering.

"Excuse me?" Her voice sounded strained.

"Mom had dinner nearly ready and you weren't home. She was wondering where you were." He crossed to the window, looked out over the porch he had yet to repair. "I thought you might be…scared or upset, so I went out to look for you."

Callie put a hand to her mouth, wide-eyed. Feeling guilty. *Good.*

"I went back to the hospital," he said, "but your mom hadn't seen you since we'd left her earlier."

Callie put a hand on the back of the couch. "You saw Mom again?"

He nodded. "I didn't tell her you'd disappeared, just that I wanted to see how she was. She was so pleased that we were married, she was...teary."

Callie looked teary herself, but Jack didn't feel any remorse. He leaned against the windowsill.

"I went by the high school, and a couple of your friends' places. I even went down to the swimming hole." The place where Lucy had drowned. Damn, it had been hard, forcing himself along that grassy path. "Unlike you, I had a cell phone. Just as I was starting to worry, Mom called to say you'd phoned and you were having dinner with a friend." His lips thinned. "I guess you didn't tell her you were having sex."

Callie was beet-red, but she no longer looked guilty. "Give it up, Jack," she snapped. "Who I make love with is none of your business, just as your girlfriends are none of mine. It wasn't a one-night stand. Rob and I dated for three years."

She'd told him that fascinating fact before, dammit. A headache pounded at Jack's temples. He put it down to the shock of discovering his wife had slept with another man on their wedding night.

Silence seethed between them.

Callie said, "Thank you."

Jack pressed his fingers to his temples. "For what?"

"For coming to look for me that day. You used to be a really nice guy."

Then she realized what she'd said, and started to laugh. Jack should have been offended. But her eyes sparkled and in the aftermath to his overly-emotional reaction to her confession, he found himself very reluctantly laughing along with her. At himself.

Beneath the humor, though, was an edge of frustration. It had been there before, since the first time he'd kissed her, but now that he knew the mysterious Rob Hanson had all the memories of her wedding night, Jack wanted Callie more then he'd have thought possible.

CHAPTER TWELVE

BRENDA CREPT INTO HER darkened bedroom. She undressed as silently as possible, felt under her pillow for her nightdress and slipped into it. She held her breath as she slid between the sheets.

"How was the bridal shower?" Dan's voice came out of the darkness, startling her.

She pressed a hand to her thudding heart. "Fine."

"Many there?"

"A dozen or so." She counted the syllables as she spoke. Envisaging words as a collection of syllables helped her strip the emotion out.

"Any problems?"

She heard the tightness in Dan's voice. "No."

They'd barely spoken to each other since he'd found her at the river the other day. Brenda was afraid that once they started talking, she would say things that couldn't be unsaid.

She yawned theatrically. "Good night, Dan."

She lay on her back, perfectly still, until she was sure he was asleep. Then, quietly, she let the tears out. It was like unblocking a sink, a blessed relief.

Suddenly Dan's bedside light flicked on, and he loomed over her. Brenda's hands fluttered to her face, but there were far too many tears for her to conceal.

He patted the pillow, which she knew would be soaked. "Dammit, Brenda, this has to stop."

She scrambled to move away from him. "I was just…it doesn't matter…I'm fine."

"You're *not* fine." He shoved a hand through his hair. "I can't take this anymore. Get some help."

"You can't take what?" She sat up. "Can't take the fact that I won't deny our daughter ever existed? That I still think about her, say her name?"

"Oh, for Pete's sake," he said. "Of course I think about her, too."

"I can't grieve for our daughter all alone, Dan. The pain is too much for one person."

His jaw jutted out, and he said tightly, "You don't have a monopoly on pain."

"You never even cried," she said. "Not once. You just accepted it."

"I don't want to cry!" he roared. "I want to feel better."

"You can't feel better if you don't feel bad to start with."

"You think because I don't break down in public, I don't feel bad?"

She fumbled on the nightstand for her glasses, put them on. "This isn't about *in public,* Dan. I can't let go of Lucy when no one else is making the effort to remember her."

"And I can't go on living like this. I'm your husband, I love you, I want our marriage back. I want a wife beside me who's not wallowing in a situation we can't change." He thumped his pillow in frustration. "I'm sick of waking up each day not knowing if this is going to be a good day or a bad day for you. It's time to move on, Brenda."

"Like you moved on? You built that damn bench, put Lucy's name on it, and somehow that let you off the hook and you never had to say her name again." Shivering in the warm room, Brenda pulled the sheet up to her chin. "After all the joy of raising our daughter, after all that pain, Lucy's life came down to a garden bench."

He stared at her, breathing heavily. "That's nuts."

"I'm sorry, Dan, I tried doing it your way—why do you think we've had years of hardly talking about Lucy? But I can't do it anymore. Not when I see Sarah getting married, and Callie making her way in the world. I wake up every morning and my mind is filled with images of what Lucy would be doing, what she would look like, if she was still here…and every night I go to bed knowing I'll never see her, never share those moments with her."

She pulled the covers over her head so that all she could hear was her own breathing. It was as if Dan wasn't there at all.

CALLIE WASN'T AT HOME when Jack arrived at the cottage the morning after they didn't make love—it was auction day. But she didn't come back from the shop at the regular time that evening, either.

She was avoiding him.

Not surprising considering his childish reaction last night.

He spent two more days slaving away at Callie's place, without one glimpse of her. Which was damned annoying. Jack had half a mind to walk off the job, if only he wasn't worried about her catching typhoid in this wreck of a house.

Who did she think was doing all this work—the elves? She had a nerve, assuming he was going to turn up each day. Taking his arrival so much for granted that she left clean rags out for him and a pot of her incredible coffee, fresh and hot when he arrived. He could get on a plane at a moment's notice and leave her to fix her own damn house.

The only reason he wasn't on that plane, he told himself, was that the weather had finally dried up. Jack had started painting the outside. It was tedious work, especially the preparation, but someone had to do it.

It wasn't all bad. He actually felt relief not having the constant pressure of patients relying on him. Not being kept awake wondering if he could have done anything differently on those occasions where the outcome wasn't what he'd hoped.

As he ran his brush along a board, Jack realized he felt more relaxed than he had in months, maybe years. When he went to Paris, he must take more time out.

Not that he'd be painting houses there, but he might find time to read the odd book on do-it-yourself projects.

The absurdity of the thought struck him, and he laughed out loud.

And wished Callie was here to share it. She always enjoyed the opportunity to laugh at him.

Maybe he should go see her, give her an update about the house and when he expected to be done. He glanced at his watch. Nearly lunchtime. Maybe he'd take her some lunch. Not junk food, but something she'd enjoy. With lettuce, if necessary. So he could apologize for acting like a jerk.

THE SIGN ON THE DOOR of Fresher Flowers said "Back in 15 minutes." Jack had been waiting in his car for twenty.

How did Callie expect business to pick up if she wasn't even here, for Pete's sake? With a muttered curse, he got out of the Jaguar. He would walk around the square, and if he didn't find her, he'd give up.

He headed west, past the souvenir shop. When he reached the furniture shop, R.H. Designs, he automatically glanced inside.

And saw Callie, wearing a flowery dress, talking to someone. She was smiling, maybe laughing—he could see her mouth in profile, her even white teeth.

Jack strode into the store.

She was chatting to a man, probably the store owner, who was—Jack's eyes narrowed—unmistakably flirting with her, his head tilted down, his tone confiding. Then the guy saw Jack; he put a hand on her upper arm.

"Excuse me," he said to her, and his thumb stroked the flesh that Jack knew was soft but firm, eminently kissable. "I have a customer."

With evident reluctance, he let go of her…and Jack's urge to knock his teeth down his throat ebbed slightly.

"Can I help you?" the guy asked.

Yeah, you can leave my wife alone.

"Jack!" Callie stepped toward them. "Rob, this is Jack Mitchell."

Rob? As in, the guy Callie had slept with the day she married Jack? Jack's right hand curled into a fist.

Was this where she'd been the past few days, while Jack was rebuilding her damn house from the ground up?

"Jack, this is an old friend of mine, Rob Hanson." It was obvious she remembered the last conversation they'd had about her "old friend," because her face turned pink.

Jack shook the guy's hand. Hanson was, he judged, good-looking to women. His build was trim and athletic, and he obviously got plenty of sun. His hair was too long, but some women seemed to like that.

"Great to meet you, Jack." Rob's handshake was firm, but not some macho challenge. "Callie's told me so much about you over the years." He slung an arm across her shoulders, giving her a squeeze. "Remember how you used to worship him back when you and I were dating, hon? In those days, Jack Mitchell could do no wrong."

"Boy, things change," she said brightly.

Jack should have been irritated after the way she'd been ignoring him the past few days, especially now he'd discovered where she was spending her time. But he felt himself begin to smile.

"So, Jack," Rob said, "you looking for anything in particular?"

My wife, he almost said. He forced himself to

ignore that Rob still had an arm around Callie, and scanned the store.

"I admire your work every time I walk by," he said, deciding to be the bigger man about this. He inspected a coffee table with beveled edges. The workmanship was flawless. "You have a tremendous talent."

"Thanks."

"I'm surprised you can make a living out of this kind of furniture in Parkvale," Jack said. *Why don't you leave town, buddy? Go somewhere a million miles away from Callie?* The heat of the sentiment surprised him, and he shoved his hands into his pockets.

"I should head to the city," Rob agreed. "But everything I love most is here."

Jack decided it was no coincidence that the guy's eyes went to Callie.

"A store in Memphis takes a few of my pieces," he continued. "That gives me enough income to get by. My workshop is out the back here, and the rent's pretty cheap."

Jack inspected a carved lamp base. "You could make a name for yourself in New York, Chicago."

Rob half laughed, half sighed. "That's the dream, of course. But making it happen..."

"You're not even trying," Callie said. "If you want something, you have to go after it. Like Jack did."

Jack stared at her. It sounded as if she admired him.

"Of course, it doesn't mean you have to leave your roots behind," she said pointedly. "Parkvale can still be your home, even if you're selling to stores in New York."

"It's hard to even figure out where to start," Rob murmured.

Jack hid a smile. He could see now why Callie had turned down Rob's marriage proposal. She'd gone to community college, trained as a florist, started her own business and renovated several houses, selling all of them at a profit. And she'd still found time to be a devoted daughter figure to Brenda and Dan. And a thorn in Jack's flesh.

Absentmindedly, she ran a hand over a fine walnut bowl, the gesture loving, sensual. Jack wanted her hands on him. He took a few steps to look at a carved bedstead, with Rob at his heels.

Callie wished Jack would leave. She'd come to visit Rob to remind herself there were other men she liked and who liked her back. To prove that the abandon she felt in Jack's arms was nothing special.

Rob was attractive, no doubt about that. Smart and nice, as she'd told Jack. He'd kissed her when she arrived, and he'd been touching her one way or another ever since.

She might as well be garbed head to toe in neoprene for all his touch did for her.

But Rob kept insisting they were meant to be together. She'd loved him once, after all.

As a schoolgirl. As a lonely young woman.

It wasn't until Jack walked into the store that her pulse had finally kicked into action, blood had rushed to her head. His masculine presence had made nice, easygoing Rob look like a pesky kitten.

Even now, Rob's words washed over her, but everything Jack said imprinted itself on her brain, which seemed to have only one purpose these days. To be a storehouse for Jack's words, for the memories of his touch, his kisses.

He wandered back in her direction, and she wiped the longing from her expression.

"You realize you've been gone from the shop a lot longer than fifteen minutes?" Jack asked. He sounded ticked off.

"You're right. I'd better get back."

"I haven't seen you in a while," he added uncertainly.

The other reason she'd been avoiding him, apart from this crazy attraction that she didn't want to indulge, was in the hope that he couldn't leave for England if he didn't see her to say goodbye. She took a deep breath and said, "Are you leaving town?"

He frowned. "What? Why would I…" Then he realized what she meant. "I decided to stay through the rest of the month."

"Really?" She'd expected to hear that he'd tried to leave but the flights were full.

He shrugged. "Seems your nagging got into my head, and if I go now I won't be able to sleep nights."

Callie's smile burst out of her; Jack's heart started beating double time. *Not possible,* he reminded himself.

"Jack, that's wonderful." She grabbed his hands, squeezing them.

"So—" Rob muscled in, no surprise there "—I hear you two are finally getting a divorce?"

"What?" Jack slammed Callie with his gaze.

"Ah. Did I mention I told Rob about our marriage?" she asked.

"No, you didn't *mention* it."

She spread her hands. "We dated for three years."

If she told him that thrilling fact one more time, Jack would hurt someone. Namely Rob.

"No big deal," she said. "You told Diana."

It took Jack a minute to remember who Diana was. She seemed so far away, she might as well be on another planet. Along with the whole of Oxford.

The only woman on his mind was Callie.

"I told her recently, under pressure to explain." He scowled. "Next time I get married it won't be to such a blabbermouth."

"Next time I get married," she retorted, "I'll be sure to choose someone who doesn't act as if he eats scalpels for breakfast."

He glared. "I'm going back to the cottage."

"Have dinner with me tomorrow night."

Callie's spontaneous offer was followed by a startled silence. Jack would bet she was more surprised than anyone.

Tomorrow? Did she know what day that was?

She smiled tentatively, and Jack pictured the two of them in an intimate restaurant, holding hands, feet touching beneath the table. Later, the long kiss good-night...

The prospect of dinner with her was a temptation he'd never faced before—and what harm could one meal do? Besides, Rob looked like a kid who'd just had his ice cream cone snatched on the hottest day of the year.

Jack said, "I'll make a reservation. It's a date."

BRENDA TURNED FROM THE stove when Callie walked into her kitchen. "Sweetie, how nice to see you." She left the meat sauce she was stirring and went to fill the kettle with water.

"I'll make the coffee," Callie said quickly. "I promise, I'll water yours down."

Brenda returned to the dinner preparations. A saucepan of potatoes boiled on the rear element. She was making Dan's favorite, shepherd's pie. She hummed a line of "A Wonderful Guy" from *South Pacific*. They'd seen the musical in Memphis back before Jack was born.

"You sound happy," Callie said.

"I'm working on it," Brenda surprised herself by saying.

"That's great." Callie hugged her. "This is the first time I've heard you admit that things aren't what you'd like them to be."

"You mean, I've been acting like a loon." Brenda tasted the meat and added a teaspoon of salt. "I keep thinking if I smile everything will be okay. Which works up to a point, but then it hits me, and I can't stop crying. Or yelling at Alvin Briggs."

"Alvin deserved it," Callie assured her.

She was a wonderful girl, Brenda thought. A true blessing to her and Dan.

"So what exactly is the *it* that hits you?" Callie asked. "I know you're thinking about Lucy, but why does it seem to hurt more now?"

Brenda put a lid on the sauce to let it simmer. "Let's sit down, sweetie."

Callie set two mugs of coffee—one light brown and one, in Brenda's opinion, pitch-black—on the pine table, and they sat.

"You remember I had counseling for depression after Lucy died," Brenda said.

Callie nodded. "Medication, too, didn't you?"

"Prozac," Brenda confirmed. "It got me through that first year. I don't know what I'd have done without it. But after that…" She picked up her mug, blew on the hot coffee

"After that?" Callie prompted.

"A year seems to be the cutoff point for acceptable grief after the death of a loved one," Brenda said. "By then, people expect you to have moved on. They certainly don't expect you to be wallowing, as Dan puts it."

"I still miss Lucy," Callie said. "I can't remember at what point the thought of her stopped bringing tears to my eyes. But then I wasn't her mother."

Brenda patted her hand. "You might have only been with us two years before she died, but you two were more sisters than a lot of other girls I've seen."

Callie smiled, blinking hard, and Brenda loved her for still caring about Lucy.

"Most of the time I was fine," Brenda said. "But there were days when I wanted to stay in bed crying. I didn't do it, of course." She sipped her coffee. "Maybe I should have."

"How did Dan feel?" Callie asked.

Brenda made a cutting motion with her hand. "As far as he was concerned, that chapter of our life was over. He didn't want to reminisce about Lucy. He's hardly said her name in five years."

"So what's changed for you?"

Brenda puffed out a breath. "I think it's seeing the girls who were Lucy's age hitting all those milestones that she never will. The past year in particular has been very difficult. I tried talking to Dan, but he didn't want to hear it…and now my feelings just keep breaking out, usually at the worst possible moments."

"Maybe you need more counseling," Callie suggested.

"Dan and I had a fight after I got back from Sarah's shower last night," Brenda said. "He was so mad, he slept on the couch in the den."

Callie's forehead wrinkled. "You make it sound as if that's a good thing."

"It is. To me, anyway." Brenda sat back. "So far he's been concerned, tolerant, maybe mildly anxious. Last night was the first time he actually said anything about how he's feeling. It's a breakthrough."

"So what happens next?"

"We talk," Brenda said simply. "It's only the first step, but it's one we have to take."

She heard the rumble of Dan's truck in the driveway, and her heart lifted. "Here he is now."

A minute later, Dan walked into the kitchen.

"Hello, darling," Brenda said.

Dan's eyes were flat, expressionless. He jerked a nod at her, gave Callie a tense smile and walked right on through to the living room. A few seconds later, the TV came on.

Brenda looked at Callie, saw her biting her lip.

"He's still angry from last night," Brenda said. "He'll come around."

"Why don't you both come for breakfast on

Saturday?" Callie said. "He'll have to talk to you if you're at my place."

"He'll be over this by then." Brenda hoped.

"I'll go ask him."

Callie was back from the living room in under a minute. "He said he needs to get an early start with inventory at the store on Saturday."

"Maybe another time, sweetie." Brenda forced a smile, then dropped it. She wasn't going to pretend everything was fine anymore.

BY THE TIME Callie got back to the cottage, she had to hurry to get ready for dinner with Jack. She hoped Brenda and Dan were having a pleasant dinner, though with Dan's uncommunicativeness it seemed unlikely. When it came to talking about Lucy, she mused as she dried her hair, it was a case of like father, like son. There must be a way to get Jack to open up about his sister.

The solution came to her as she finished dressing, just as Jack rang the doorbell.

Callie had seen Jack in paint-stained denims and ragged T-shirts so often, he was almost a stranger— an intimidating stranger—in his dark, pressed pants, crisp striped shirt and light gray sports jacket.

Was she crazy, suggesting dinner? She'd been so pleased to learn he was staying in town, she'd wanted to…reward him. As if dinner with her was such a great reward!

Though the way his eyes heated as he scanned her green halter-neck dress, maybe it was.

"You look amazing," he said. He kissed her lightly

on the lips, then deliberately released her. As always, she wanted more.

Too bad she'd had an idea that would make this dinner less reward for him, more torture.

CHAPTER THIRTEEN

"WHAT WOULD YOU SAY if I suggested we have fast food tonight?" she asked.

"I'd say you're a woman after my own heart." Then, obviously realizing how unlikely that was, he added, "What's the catch?"

"I want to eat my fast food down by the river."

He stiffened. "Forget it. I made reservations, and we'll be a lot more comfortable at Brunello." He folded his arms. "You don't even like fast food."

"Please, Jack." She looked up at him through lowered lashes.

He gazed down at her hand for a long moment. He shook his head, but the word that came out was, "Okay."

Callie had to believe he knew what day this was, and that was why he'd agreed. But if he didn't, she wasn't about to complicate matters. "Could you grab the blanket from the hall closet?" she said. "I have a bottle of wine in the fridge, and I'll bring some glasses."

They drove through Burger King on their way, and carried their paper bags to the river. Callie spread the blanket.

He sat down after she did. She noticed he'd turned his back to the river.

"Thank you for agreeing to come here," she said.

He busied himself pouring the wine. She took the glass he offered, clinked it against his.

"Happy Anniversary," he said.

"You remembered!" Just like that, she got a lump in her throat. Which was beyond stupid. They'd never been a couple, so what did their anniversary matter?

"Don't tell me you weren't relying on that to persuade me to come here." But he didn't sound angry.

"I did think you might find it appropriate," she admitted.

He glanced over his shoulder at the clear, rushing water, then back again. "If Lucy hadn't died, we wouldn't be having this anniversary."

Callie became pensive. "You wouldn't be back in Parkvale now, either. If we hadn't got married, you wouldn't have come home for a divorce."

"Which it turns out I didn't need to do," he pointed out.

"You'd already decided to come back, to check on me."

He nodded.

"Look at the river, Jack," she said. "Take a good look."

"I've seen it before."

"It's just water. It's not even the same water that killed Lucy."

He made an impatient motion with his hand.

"She loved it here," Callie said. "We came down nearly every day during the summer. When I look at this river, I remember her laughing and fooling around. Her competitive streak, always wanting to see who could jump in fastest, hold their breath longest."

He smiled. "That sounds like Lucy."

To Callie's surprise, he turned to look at the water. She scooted over next to him, and he slung an arm across her shoulders. They watched the river flow by, the muted rush of the current the only sound.

"I guess that wasn't so scary," Jack said. He squeezed her shoulder. "I just didn't want to be reminded…. In my job I see a lot of sick kids, and some of them don't pull through. I try not to think about them."

"But it's not easy," Callie suggested, remembering his obvious affection for Hannah.

"I wish I could flip a switch and no longer care."

Callie shifted even closer so she was nestled against him. "I'm glad you can't. You loved Lucy, so it's right that you should find this hard. And you care about your patients, so you worry about them." For the first time, she could see why he might not want to worry about his parents, why he might be in denial about their need for him.

"Maybe you should find someone you can share this stuff with," she said. "A wife." She moved out of his embrace to open the food. She handed him his burger.

"Wives are too much work," he said. "Mine won't let me be anything less than a saint."

"I thought you already were a saint, in your estimation." She unwrapped her own burger.

His wry smile said she'd scored a point. "If I did

want to get married again, how long should I wait after the divorce?"

"Given the nature of our marriage, I don't think you need to wait at all," she said coolly.

"Hey, a lot of marriages don't last as long as ours. I don't want to disrespect that."

"We did have a good track record," she reflected. "Not talking to each other for eight years probably helped."

"Yeah." He bit into his burger. "I wonder where I'll find another woman who doesn't need me to talk to her."

"Doctor, Doctor," Callie muttered, "my husband's a jerk."

Jack quirked an eyebrow, waiting.

"There's no punch line," she said crossly. "It's not funny."

So of course, he laughed. "That's the funniest doctor joke I ever heard."

"Maybe you just can't help being a jerk," she said. "Maybe it's a medical condition."

"I haven't heard of it." He paused as he studied her. "You, of course, are not a jerk at all. In fact, you're quite lovely."

Darned seductive British compliments! "Save it for your next wife."

His eyes crinkled disarmingly. "Jealous?"

"Whoever it is will probably only be interested in your salary," Callie lied. She took a generous sip of wine. "And, yeah, we're all jealous of that. So if you have a rich doctor friend you can introduce me to after we get divorced…"

His eyes flashed. He tugged a blade of grass from the ground and leaned back on one elbow, laconic yet alert. "I think you *are* jealous."

She snorted and used her finger to get the last grains of salt from her now-empty bag of fries. "Mmm."

"The thing is," Jack said slowly, "you might not be jealous of my future wife, but I'm jealous as hell of Rob."

Her eyes widened. "Rob does have a great haircut," she agreed.

He flicked his napkin at her.

They were silent for a long moment before she ventured to say, "You don't need to be jealous of Rob."

His eyes darkened. "You mean, my haircut's as good as his?"

"I think your haircut is a lot better than his."

Callie was breathing such rarefied air now, she was in danger of hyperventilating.

Good thing she was with a doctor.

A doctor who wanted her. She wanted him right back, and she was sick of denying it. *He's my husband.* She banished the image of Casey and Adam Carmichael. Not everyone had that kind of marriage.

Jack's thumb found the tender inside of her wrist, drew gentle circles. "This is our last anniversary. How about we make it one to remember?" He lifted her hand to his mouth, kissed her fingertips. Callie moaned.

Jack crumpled his napkin. "Let's get out of here."

She let him tug her to her feet.

NEITHER OF THEM SAID a word on the way home, for fear of breaking the mood. Or, in Callie's case, for fear of whimpering with desire and revealing to Jack just how desperate she was.

How had she reached this pathetic state? she wondered as, lips clamped together, she got out of the car without waiting for Jack to open her door. Then he took her hand to drag her up the back steps, and just that touch caused atoms to collide inside her.

Oh yeah, that's how.

She fumbled in her purse, searching for her key. He grabbed the bag from her and dumped the contents on the doorstep, thank goodness, so he could lay his hands on the key faster. Pushing the door open, he gave Callie a little shove over the threshold, then bent to scoop up all the clutter from her purse, including her copy of the divorce papers.

Don't think about it.

Jack dropped the paraphernalia on the counter. "You have been driving me crazy the past two weeks," he said huskily.

There was a light in his eyes that definitely could be insanity, if only she was qualified to diagnose it. On the other hand, it could be raw, powerful desire. The kind no woman could resist.

It's not love.

Damn, why did I think that? She wasn't looking for love from Jack, but if she didn't *make love* to him right now, she might die of frustration.

He ran his hands lightly down her arms, and she shivered. Then he lost all patience and hauled her into a hard embrace. His mouth covered hers and she gave herself up to him.

The back of her head bumped against the fridge,

and Jack's murmur of apology was lost in the tangle of their mouths. He pushed her dress up so he could cup her bottom, and she pressed against him until he groaned.

"Bedroom," he ordered, and walked her backward down the hall, almost carrying her. They made it into her romantic, over-the-top boudoir, which now seemed to have been created for just this moment. In a distant corner of her mind, Callie registered the rasp of her zipper, the slide of her dress down her body, Jack's incredible hands touching her bra, her panties.

Then he released her, stepping back so he could see her. "Wow," he said reverently.

Callie glanced down, knew a moment of panic. "I'm naked."

Jack grinned. "Yeah, it's my lucky night."

Her embarrassment melted in the heat of his gaze, and she laughed. "I want to get lucky, too," she said boldly.

It took Jack all of ten seconds to strip off his clothes…every scrap.

"Wow." She borrowed his word, though it didn't do him justice. "You are sooo not impotent."

"There was never any doubt," he said sternly. He started to swat her backside, but it turned into an intimate caress.

Callie feasted with her eyes as he led her to the bed. He pulled her down beside him and took her mouth in another of those overpowering kisses, while his hands roamed her body, building her excitement to a fever pitch. She couldn't get enough of his lips, his palms, the muscular feel of him beneath her fingers.

With a groan, he moved over her.

She tugged on his hair. "Slow down. You're going too fast."

He ran his hands over her again, felt her shudder. He nipped her shoulder. "I'm ready, you're ready, what's the problem?"

"I want to enjoy this." She gasped as his mouth moved lower.

He gave half a laugh. "You'll enjoy it, I guarantee."

Then, before she could protest—and, really, how could she protest about the incredible sensation of Jack's body joining to hers?—he claimed her.

"THAT WAS INCREDIBLE." Jack's voice was a deep rumble against Callie's neck.

"Incredibly *fast*," she said. She couldn't believe it. Probably the one and only time she'd go to bed with Jack Mitchell, and it had been all over in five minutes.

Admittedly, five *glorious* minutes.

"Hey!" He propped himself up on one elbow, and his gaze roved over her body. His other hand headed for her waist. "You enjoyed that as much as I did."

She sighed. "I might have known you'd make love as efficiently as you do everything else."

He ceased his slow stroking of her abdomen, and she shivered at the withdrawal. "Are you saying it wasn't good?" He sounded annoyed, which wasn't unexpected.

"It was lovely," she said quietly. Understatement. She hadn't wanted it to end, and was annoyed that he'd insisted on setting the pace. "But definitely too fast. Call it an, uh, artistic disagreement."

A flush spread along his jawline. "That was not too fast. And I'm telling you, sex doesn't get any better than that, fast or slow."

Callie put space between them in the bed. "Can't you admit that maybe you don't know everything?" She'd thought he was learning to consider others' points of view, but this felt eerily like his first few days back in Parkvale. Except for the naked bit.

"Can't you not argue for once?" He shoved the covers aside and got out of bed. Callie looked away while he grabbed his pants and stepped into them. "I know damn well you enjoyed it," he said. "But I'll bet that right now your brain is trying to turn the fact that we went a bit faster than you wanted—which, by the way, isn't unusual for a guy the first time he makes love to a woman he's been wanting—into evidence that I don't care about others."

"Maybe I'm thinking that way because it's true." She rushed from the bed to snatch her robe, but Jack wasn't even looking.

"I don't have to prove to you that I love my family," he said.

Callie belted the robe. "Sure you love them, in the big picture. I'm talking about the love that means being a part of each other's lives. Not every day, but knowing that if you call the other person, they're happy to hear from you. It's about sharing life's little moments. Being able to laugh together about the time Uncle Frank fell off the roof while he was helping Dan paint the house, and landed smack bang on the trampoline."

"You weren't there then," he said, confused.

"Exactly," she replied impatiently. "It's *your* memory, not mine. Your parents told me about it, but you're the only one who can share it with them. I can't reminisce about how your mom invented Parkvale Curried Chicken Salad so she could whip the pastor's wife in the International Supper Club cook-off. I've heard the story, but I don't even remember what the pastor's wife made."

"Gazpacho," Jack said. "She should have known a chilled soup wouldn't cut it in Parkvale."

"See?" Callie straightened the sheets, trying to remove all evidence of their activity. "That's exactly what I mean."

"No, I don't see." Jack took the other side of the bed; he snapped the sheet in frustration.

"I can't laugh about how Lucy used to call you Yak before she could say your name properly," Callie said. "Or...or how she spied on you and one of your dates and repeated the whole conversation, complete with actions, to your parents the next day. Or how—"

"That's enough," he ordered. "Just because I went to the damn river with you, you don't get to drag Lucy into our fights. None of that stuff you're talking about matters."

He stalked across the room to pick up his shirt from next to the dresser, where it had landed when he stripped off at the speed of light.

As he buttoned it, he scanned the photographs on her dresser—pictures of Callie with her mom, with Lucy, with Rob, with Brenda and Dan. In the drawer below, though he didn't know it, was the photo from their wedding day.

He turned, and there was a disconcerting, knowing look in his eyes.

"You tell me nonstop that I need to get more involved in my family," he said. "But what about *your* family?"

"I don't have one," she said, confused.

"I know you want one. You want to get married, have kids, build a family of your own, but you're not doing a damn thing about it."

The words twisted like a knife. "I can't manufacture a family…"

"You turned down Rob when he wanted to marry you, and, hell, I can see that was a smart decision. But as far as I can tell you don't date—and don't give me any garbage about being married to me, because we both know that wouldn't stop you if you found the right guy. As far as I know, you haven't had any really close friends since Lucy, you've never tried to find out what happened to your father, you made one attempt to contact your grandparents—"

"They turned me down!"

"So why the hell didn't you jump on the next plane to California and confront them?" He paced across the room. "Why aren't you dating? You know exactly what a family should be like, and you're putting all your effort into making it happen in *my* family."

She fisted her hands at her sides. "I love your parents. I want them to be happy."

"You love them and they love you, but my family is never *about* you," he said. "You're the one helping out, the one on the sidelines."

"Stop it!" Callie snapped.

"Even your job is about being on the sidelines at other people's birthdays, weddings, christenings."

"Shut *up!*"

"Who sends you flowers?" he asked abruptly. "Who sends flowers to the florist?"

She paled, bit her lip. "I...no one," she whispered.

His silence said, *I told you so.*

"It would be stupid to send flowers to a florist," she said desperately.

Still he said nothing.

"Just because you cut people's brains open, it doesn't give you the inside track on my mind."

He stared her down. "The Mitchells are my family," he said. "Get your own."

AFTER JACK LEFT, Callie wandered the cottage in her robe, looking at all her hard work, and Jack's, and had the depressing realization that, much as she loved it, this cottage did not, in itself, give her everything she needed in a home. She'd spent the eight years since her mother died trying to create a haven for herself, some kind of security. But she'd been so busy focusing on the physical—the material—she'd forgotten she wanted more.

Jack was wrong to say Dan and Brenda weren't hers. They loved Callie—they didn't consider her a second-class member of the family. But she did hold a part of herself back, a part she was saving for a relationship more intimate than any she'd known.

Yet, right now, she wasn't even trying to pursue such a relationship. Jack was right about that, at least. Since when had he been so insightful?

Since she'd opened her heart to him.

Fallen in love with him.

No way. She tried to backpedal, but it was one of those thoughts you can't take back. Instead, it swelled to fill her head and her heart.

I love Jack.

Callie sagged onto the couch in the living room he'd turned into a cozy, welcoming space. She put her fist to her mouth, bit on her knuckles as she tried to make sense of it all.

Jack was a pompous, self-important jerk with no respect for his roots, who'd left her to handle his parents while he built a brilliant career. But he was also a man who cared deeply for his patients, who wanted to do the right thing, even if he was somewhat screwed up about what the right thing was.

He'd been furious at Callie about her refusal to sign the divorce papers, yet he'd never been less than respectful.

Maybe she'd fallen in love with Jack because, as he said, she was too afraid to go after the family she wanted. That would make sense, he didn't love her back and he was about to leave town. There was no risk that in loving him she'd actually have to do something about it.

That's not why I love him. She loved him for his drive and determination. For his decency. For the protectiveness he tried to deny, but which showed up at every turn. For the way he heard her views and, however reluctantly, did the right thing. For his sense of humor, for his gorgeous body. And because he was Jack.

JACK FELT LIKE a louse the next morning as he sat at his parents' kitchen table, making calls to colleagues in Oxford while his mom fixed him the cooked breakfast she insisted he needed.

He and Callie had had incredible sex—no matter what she said about *too fast*—and he'd thanked her by telling her to get a life.

He'd meant every word.

Callie was made to have a family. It was nuts that she didn't.

Jack tossed his cell phone on the table and thought about how devastated she'd looked when he'd left last night. For the first time, he wondered if they'd done the right thing, cutting her grandparents out of her life.

Were they the manipulators Callie's mom had believed them to be? And if they had been, had they mellowed with age? Callie had said her grandfather had refused to accept her attempt at contact. But...

Jack felt as if he owed Callie a family of her own. Especially now that he'd made love with her. He wouldn't be her husband much longer, and he wasn't the guy to build a family with her...but he could still help.

"Jack, could you ask your father if he wants white toast or sourdough?" his mom asked.

Jack glanced at his father, sitting at the other end of the table reading the paper. "Uh, he's right here, Mom."

A frying pan clattered on the stove. "Yes, but he's not speaking to me until I'm prepared to 'be reasonable,'" Brenda said. She spoke lightly, but even someone as ill-attuned to his parents' needs as Jack was—according to Callie—could discern the hurt beneath the words.

Dan rattled the paper in front of his face.

Jack sighed. "Dad, do you want white toast or sourdough?"

"White," he said.

"Did you get that, Mom?"

Another clatter came from the stove.

Uh-oh.

AFTER HIS DAD LEFT for the shop and his mom for her book group, Jack made a couple more calls back to England. But he couldn't rid himself of his speculation about Callie's grandparents.

Jack called Sam Magill and asked for a recommendation on a private investigator. Sam put him onto Mark Haines, whose calm, professional manner inspired confidence. Jack explained the situation.

"I'd like you to track down William and Mona Summers," he concluded. "Find out what kind of people they are, if they might welcome renewed contact with their granddaughter. I don't want to risk her getting hurt again."

That sounded sappy, but Haines didn't seem to notice. "You have any address details, any photos?"

"No photos, but they were living in Monterey."

One of the most expensive parts of California. Callie's mom had said her in-laws were rich.

"Should be easy enough," Haines said. "Hopefully, I can do it within a week."

When Jack put down the phone, he was still dissatisfied. Dammit, there was nothing else he could do for Callie. Nothing that didn't ask more than he was willing to give.

CHAPTER FOURTEEN

CALLIE'S PHONE RANG at one in the morning on Tuesday, two days after she and Jack had made love.

Bad news. She jerked upright, reached for the phone on the nightstand, fumbled it, then lifted it to her ear.

"Mom went out fifteen minutes ago," Jack said. "We don't know where."

"Did you try the bathroom?" Callie asked groggily.

That was met with a patient silence.

The fog in her brain cleared, and she snapped to attention. "Sorry, I'm awake now."

"Dad and I thought you might have some idea where she is," Jack said. "She took her car."

Callie tucked the phone between her ear and shoulder. She scrambled out of bed, began pulling on the clothes she'd removed a couple of hours earlier. "Did she take anything? A bag?"

"I don't think so."

Callie's mind raced. "Maybe the river."

"That's what we thought," Jack said. "We're going to look for her. We'll swing by and pick you up."

"I'm ready," she said.

There was heard a muffled shout from Jack's end

of the line. "Hang on." She heard him call out to his father, then he came back on. "Dad says the toolshed door is open. He's gone to check if anything's missing. We'll see you in five."

It was nearer ten minutes before Dan's Ranger pulled up, Jack at the wheel. Callie climbed in almost before he'd stopped, which earned a disapproving look from him. Since they'd made love, since he'd told her what a loser she was, she'd gone back to leaving the cottage before he arrived, and working late. This was the first time she'd seen him in two days.

She squelched a wave of hostility. They needed to find Brenda.

He didn't immediately pull out onto the road. "We have to figure out where we're going."

"Not the river?"

Dan cleared his throat. "It looks as if Brenda did take something with her. My chainsaw. I can't think of anything she'd want to cut down there."

Callie cupped her suddenly cold face with her hands. Even if Brenda wasn't doing something odd with the chainsaw—though what could she be doing at this time of night that wasn't odd?—Callie wasn't sure she knew how to use it safely.

She realized both men were watching her, waiting for direction. She closed her eyes. *Brenda, where are you?*

She opened her eyes again. "The high school."

BRENDA'S CAR WAS PARKED inside the school grounds. Jack pulled up alongside. When they got out, Dan heard it immediately—the angry buzz of a chainsaw slicing through wood.

He swore as he started jogging toward the quadrangle. Jack and Callie caught up with him and they rounded the administration building together...and stopped.

Security lighting, triggered by Brenda's movements, bathed the quadrangle.

The Lucy Mitchell Memorial Bench had been sliced into pieces. Brenda was balanced precariously on a large chunk, cutting through a section of the carved back. Sawdust flew around her, and in the light it looked like a fine drizzle of rain.

Dan ran forward, stumbling and slipping on the dew-damp grass. He was aware his mouth was moving, but he couldn't hear himself over the roar of the chainsaw.

Brenda wasn't even wearing goggles, dammit, or gloves. If she slipped, or if the saw got too heavy, she'd—

Then the enormity of what she was doing hit him. She had destroyed Lucy's bench. His heart pounded like a jackhammer. The chainsaw stopped, and he realized he was yelling, an incoherent roar of rage and grief and despair.

Brenda turned and dropped the chainsaw; it thudded on to the pile of broken wood. "Dan..."

He ignored her, just as he had the past few days. Which must have been why she'd done this. She'd insisted they had to talk, but he'd refused to let one word past his lips until she agreed to stop moping about Lucy. She'd yelled at him tonight, and he'd turned the TV up. In hindsight, it wasn't the smartest thing he'd ever done.

He reached the destruction and dropped to his knees, only too aware of the smell he'd always liked. Fresh-sawn timber.

"Lucy…" He wrapped his fingers around a loose slat. Some benches were made with off-cuts or with the cheaper, outer wood. But Dan had cut each of these slats from heartwood, matching the grain so that when you looked at the bench as a whole it had a ripple effect.

He pushed more slats aside, found one carved arm. He traced the leaf pattern with his fingers. At first glance all the leaves looked the same, but up close you could see the differences: here was the perfect-shaped leaf of a white ash, next to it the flat-bottomed cottonwood leaf, then the rounder basswood. When Dan thought of Lucy, he thought of a summer breeze through the trees. Not exactly sensible, but she'd always flitted about—one second here, the next gone, and then she was back again, laughing and loving.

"Lucy Lucy Lucy Lucy." Dan tossed pieces of wood aside, digging through the wreckage with his hands as if he might find her in there somewhere.

Dimly, he was aware of Brenda.

"Dan." She sounded frightened. "I'm sorry, I was so angry, I…lost it."

He kept digging, but he couldn't see properly. Brenda said to someone, "He's crying." Was he? He didn't know, didn't care.

Jack got down beside him, started combing through the broken bits of bench, not saying a word. Dan realized Jack's actions weren't random; he was sorting the pieces of wood. There wasn't any reason to do it, but that seemed like a good idea.

"Dan, I'm sorry," Brenda repeated.

If he spoke to her right now, his heart might explode. Head bowed to his task, Dan muttered to Jack, "Get her away from me."

Jack moved back, and Dan heard him talking to Callie.

"I'll take her to my place," she said.

Then the women were gone, and it was just Dan and Jack, sifting, sorting.

"I'll bring the truck around, and we'll load it up," Jack said when they had three neat piles.

"Not much point. This isn't fit for anything more than a bonfire." Dan's voice wobbled. He jammed his hands in his pockets and ducked his head.

"I'll bring the truck," Jack said.

BRENDA STAYED at Callie's place the whole of the next day. Jack didn't work on the cottage; he spent the time trying to iron out the mess his mom had made. He was exhausted by the time he reached Callie's at six o'clock.

He drove Brenda home.

"You have to face Dad sooner or later," he said as they turned into Stables Lane. "You owe it to him to make it sooner."

Brenda knotted her fingers in her lap. "Is he still furious with me?"

"Yep." He pulled in behind Dan's truck. "I've smoothed things over with the school, but I can't make your peace with Dad."

"How can I make peace if he won't discuss it?" Brenda asked miserably as she got out of the car.

"If there's one thing he learned last night, it's that refusing to talk can be dangerous," Jack said. "I think you'll find he's relatively chatty."

Brenda gulped as the front door opened and Dan emerged. He stood, arms akimbo, watching her approach.

"Hello, Dan," she said.

His mouth worked, then he said, "Brenda."

She looked relieved, though Jack couldn't see one word was much of an improvement over not talking. Maybe it was that Dan's tone was subdued.

His father stepped aside and Brenda entered the house. "You coming in?" he asked Jack.

"I'd rather not," Jack admitted. "You okay without me?"

"Think I can handle it." Something that might have been a glimmer of a smile crossed Dan's face. "I locked up the chainsaw."

Jack didn't need any further encouragement to go back to Callie's.

"I thought you'd like an update on the situation," he said as he strolled into her kitchen.

She studied his face. He knew he had dark circles under his eyes. So did she. Like him, she probably hadn't got back to sleep last night. "You mean, you wanted to get away from the battlefield."

"That, too," he admitted.

But before he could say anything else, his cell phone beeped. He pulled out the display. "Jeremy," he said. "It's the middle of the night over there." He felt sick at the thought of more bad news.

But this was just a minor "emergency." Hannah

was wide awake during Jeremy's night shift, and she was downhearted. She wanted Dr. Jack to cheer her up.

"Hey, Hannah." Jack forced brightness into his voice, even though he knew the struggles Jeremy was having with the bleeding in her brain. Every time they removed one source, another seemed to appear.

Hannah chattered away for a minute or so, with Jack supplying occasional uh-huhs. The conversation dwindled, and she started speculating about her health, in a way that wasn't constructive.

"I'm very hopeful that after the next operation we'll have found all those clusters," Jack said.

His smile was pained as he spoke to Hannah, and Callie realized the effort it cost him to reassure a child who daily faced death. She wondered if that was why he'd been distracted.

"Uh, sure," he said hesitantly into the phone. He put his hand over the mouthpiece and said to Callie, "Hannah wants me to tell her a joke."

She nodded encouragement.

"You know I take myself way too seriously to crack any jokes," he said. "Help me out here."

"Only if I can make it a Doctor, Doctor joke," she said.

He rolled his eyes and uncovered the phone. "Hannah, I have a, er, friend here who's really good at jokes. She's going to give me one to pass on to you."

Every joke Callie had ever heard flew out of her head under the pressure.

"Doctor, doctor," she said slowly, "I think I'm a dog."

Jack repeated it into the phone, then raised his eyebrows.

"Sit on the couch and tell me about it," Callie said in a doctor voice, growing more confident. Then, in the patient voice, "I can't, I'm not allowed on the furniture."

Jack snorted, then told the rest of the joke to the girl. From the wide smile on his face, Callie figured Hannah liked it.

Amazing how such a corny joke could give so much pleasure. And who would have thought that high-and-mighty Dr. Jack Mitchell would ever lower himself to tell it?

He had never been as lovable in Callie's eyes as he was at that moment.

When he'd finished his call, he pulled out a bar stool from the island and sat.

"Tell me how your folks are," Callie said.

He rubbed his hands over his face. "I spent the whole day shuttling between the sheriff and the school, trying to convince Principal Smith and Alvin Briggs there was no gain from having Mom arrested. They agreed at about five o'clock tonight"

"That's great news—you deserve a beer." She got one from the fridge, opened it for him.

Gratefully, he took a swallow.

"I told Mom she needs to get help, go back to counseling."

"Did you tell your father the same thing?" Callie pulled an open bottle of white wine from the fridge and poured herself a glass.

He frowned. "Dad doesn't need—" He broke off,

then said, "Maybe he does." He closed his eyes briefly. "Hell, I can't see how they're going to work this out."

He sounded so dispirited, Callie wanted to smooth the lines of fatigue at the corners of his mouth. To kiss away the tension that held him rigid, resisting the relaxing effects of the beer.

"How was Dan when Brenda got home?" She sipped her wine.

"Still quiet, but I think he's realized he and Mom need to talk." Jack started to chuckle.

"What's so funny?"

"Need to talk." He was laughing now, though there was a manic edge to it. "Need lobotomies, more like it."

"Hey, these are the people who gave you your DNA. Anything they've done, you could end up doing."

"Hell, that's scary. If you ever see me with a chain-saw, lock me away."

She saluted. "Yes, Doctor." She loved seeing him relax, hated the thought of sending him back to his parents' place where goodness knows what was going on. Maybe he should stay the night here.

With me.

The thought took instant, irrevocable hold in Callie's mind. No matter that she was still furious with Jack over the things he'd said, she still wanted him. Still felt every glance from those gray eyes as a physical touch, still wanted to kiss him every time his mouth moved. Wanted to comfort him and ease the strain he was feeling now.

Most of all, she loved him, and she badly wanted to make love with him again.

She set her wine down on the island. "Jack." The word came out unintentionally husky.

"Uh-huh?" He was still smiling. She decided to try to maintain the light mood. Not let this get too serious. Besides, he was extra gorgeous when he smiled.

"I need a doctor," she said.

Evidently she'd said that without a trace of seduction, because Jack plunked his beer down beside her wineglass. "What's the matter?" His tone was all concern, nothing loverlike.

She swung her hips as she walked around the island toward him.

He frowned. "Is there something wrong with your leg?"

Good grief, hadn't they got beyond that thing where he found a physical problem for her every emotional need? *This isn't emotional*—she caught her own faux pas—*this is physical.* Jack just had the wrong diagnosis.

She undid the top button of her blouse as she moved, and her eyes must have given away her intention.

"Uh, Callie…" His gaze was on her fingers as they moved down to the next button. It seemed he couldn't say anything else.

She was right in front of him now, close enough for him to touch. If he wanted to. "I *need* a doctor," she said in a helpless female voice.

She'd undone two buttons, and now she went for number three. She slipped it through the hole, but held the front of her blouse together and said a little breathlessly, "You *are* a doctor, right?"

She saw the moment Jack decided to play along. He stuck his thumbs in the waistband of his jeans, flexed those pecs and drawled, "Yes, ma'am, I sure am."

CHAPTER FIFTEEN

"THAT'S SUCH A RELIEF," Callie said. "I would just hate to be taking my clothes off for no good reason."

"Now, why don't you let me help you with that?" he said kindly. He made quick work of the rest of her buttons and peeled her blouse off. He surveyed her, and smiled. "Hmm, yes, I can see you are definitely in need of a doctor."

He took a step closer, put his hands on her hips.

"My, what capable hands you have, Doctor," she cooed, already turned on beyond her own imagining.

He moved those capable hands up her body, setting her tingling. "I'm afraid I don't have my stethoscope with me, ma'am, so I'm just going to have to do this by feel."

"You do what you have to, Doctor," she said bravely.

He claimed her mouth as his hands roamed her curves. But before the kiss could deepen, he pulled away.

"I can't believe I'm saying this," he said, the drawl gone. "But the doctor-patient thing isn't going to work."

Callie folded her arms across her chest, mortified.

"If you didn't want me you might have said something before I—"

He put a hand over her mouth. "Of course I want you. Are you crazy? You're killing me." He glanced down at her again, willing her to unfold her arms. Callie found herself complying. He groaned and said, "It's just, at medical school you spend so many years being told you can never, ever get involved with a patient, I just can't block the voice in my head telling me this is unethical."

"You do realize," Callie said, "that I'm a doctor, too."

He blinked. "I didn't know that."

"When I said I needed a doctor, I meant for a second opinion."

"Ah." He grinned, tugged her close again. "Well, that's an entirely different matter, Doctor. Anything to help a colleague." He took her mouth again, and the heat built quickly. Having been here before, they had some idea of the feel and taste of each other, of the excitement to come, and it lent anticipation to the kiss.

Callie pulled away before they both lost control. "You're going to need to consider this case very carefully, Dr. Mitchell. No rushing your opinion."

He swatted her backside and gave her a warning growl, but was too turned on to protest further.

Callie began unbuttoning his shirt.

"What kind of doctor are you?" he asked as he undid the zipper on her skirt.

Callie swept his shirt aside, ran her hands over his torso. "Uh…"

"Chest physician," he suggested.

"Mmm, that's it." She let him push her down onto the couch, but kept up her exploration of every curve of muscle and sinew. "Your chest is in excellent shape, by the way."

He nuzzled her neck. "From an authority like yourself, that's quite a compliment."

She squirmed against the tickling delight of his kiss, then moaned as his tongue glided the length of her collarbone.

"I'm no expert," he murmured, "but your chest appears to be a fine specimen, too."

"Thank you, Doctor." She gasped as his tongue found the hollow at the base of her neck.

He trailed kisses tantalizingly lower…then lifted his mouth to ask, "So, Doctor, where did you go to school?"

"On the Internet." She gripped his bare shoulders, ready to scream with desire, and said through clenched teeth, "That counts, doesn't it?"

"Oh, yeah," he said with a smile of supreme satisfaction, "that definitely counts." And he lowered his mouth to her again.

"THE GREAT THING ABOUT making love with a world-famous neurosurgeon," Callie said conversationally as they shared pizza in bed later, "is that you guys are such quick learners."

"What, all of us?" Jack licked a piece of mozzarella off her finger, then held her finger in his mouth while his tongue swirled around the tip.

Callie waited until she'd enjoyed the sensation to the max. "I'm assuming you're as smart as the rest of your colleagues."

"Smarter," he corrected her.

"My mistake."

"And what exactly was I so quick to learn?" he asked.

As if he didn't know! "The art," she said, "of taking things slowly. You know you enjoyed that more than last time."

"Did I?"

"And so did I," she continued. As she reached for another piece of pizza the sheet she was holding in place slipped. Jack eyed her with interest.

"Whatever you were talking about," he said, "it's time to stop."

He held her slice of pizza to her mouth while she took a bite, then demolished the rest himself in two large mouthfuls.

"Hey!" she said around her pepperoni and mushrooms.

"You know you don't like fast food."

"And you like it too much." She swallowed her mouthful. "What's that about?"

He reached under the sheet for her. "I'm ready for dessert."

She grabbed his hand. "Not until you tell me about your junk food fetish."

"It tastes good," he said. "So I eat it."

"I thought doctors like to eat healthily."

He sighed. "They do, mostly. I eat plenty of healthy food, but sometimes—often—I like to let go of that sense of…responsibility…for doing the right thing. Somehow it seems to lighten the burden of care."

Tears pricked Callie's eyes. "I'll never nag you about your diet again."

"I should be so lucky." He pushed her back into the pillows. "Time for another consultation, Doctor."

She gasped as his hands moved swiftly down her body, on target for their destination. "You're not trying to set another speed record, are you?"

"You'll soon find out." And he proceeded to show her that he had indeed learned a thing or two from her about pacing.

Later in the night, the kidding around stopped and he made love to her slowly, tenderly.

Later still, he showed her that brilliant neurosurgeons could add stamina to the list of their talents.

CALLIE ACHED ALL OVER in the best kind of way. The pleasant fatigue of muscles used in lovemaking, the heavy eyes of a night that had been short on sleep for all the right reasons, deep, contented breathing she wasn't sure was hers or Jack's...

And another sound... Scrabbling? The rats were back! She wasn't leaving this room until Jack had made sure they were all in the basement with the door locked. Hmm, an excuse to stay right here... She turned over in a drowsy haze and snuggled into Jack, reluctant to disturb him or to start a new day where, surely, they were going to have to talk about what they'd done.

Outside, cicadas chirped and above it she heard the caw of a crow. Next to the bed, Callie's clock radio played "I Got You, Babe" softly—she'd obviously left the alarm set from yesterday, but it hadn't been loud enough to waken her. Beyond the bedroom, voices filtered from the hallway—

Voices!

Callie sprang upright. "Jack!" She grabbed his shoulder, shook it. "Someone's here."

"Huh?" He opened his eyes, blinked at her.

"I thought it was rats," Callie said. Which had the effect of making him look adorably confused.

Callie heard Brenda, right outside the door, say, "I must have left it in here last night."

"It's your mom," Callie whispered. Brenda must have used the spare key to let herself in. She'd probably knocked and Callie hadn't heard... Who was she talking to?

"Have you seen what Callie's done in the master bedroom?" Brenda continued. "It's wonderful."

Callie stared at Jack and he stared back, both of them aware that Brenda would *not* consider what Callie had just done in the master bedroom at all wonderful.

"Tell her you're getting changed," Jack ordered.

"Brenda," Callie called. "I'm—"

Then the door handle turned and Callie only just had time to pull the sheet up.

"Callie! Sweetie, I thought you must have gone to the shop early—" Brenda shrieked when she saw Jack.

"What's up?" Dan elbowed past his wife. He went beet-red when he saw Callie, and glanced hastily away. Which took his gaze right to his son.

"Jack?" he said, shocked. "What the hell is going on?"

Jack sat up, which threatened to dislodge Callie's sheet. She gripped it tighter.

"Dad, Mom," he said, "could you give us a minute?"

"I can't believe it," Brenda said. She looked so upset that Callie wanted to burst into tears. "I can't believe you took advantage of Callie. You ought to be ashamed of yourself, Jack Daniel Mitchell!"

This was ludicrous—Jack getting the blame after Callie had seduced him. "Brenda," she said. "it's not like—"

"And when you're done being ashamed of yourself, you'd better name a wedding date," Dan growled. "No man treats Callie like this—"

"We're already married," Callie blurted.

Her announcement was more effective than a bucket of cold water. Both Dan and Brenda froze.

Jack groaned, and Callie realized she'd just made things a whole lot worse.

Breathing heavily—how was his blood pressure? Callie wondered—Dan said, "You two have some explaining to do. Get dressed and get out into the living room. You have two minutes."

Brenda was smiling and laughing and crying and confused. "Married! But how—? I don't believe it."

"Come along, Brenda." Dan tugged her from the room.

"Why the hell did you say that?" Jack demanded as they scrambled out of bed. He dragged on last night's pants, and Callie tried not to notice he'd chosen to go commando.

"They caught us in bed together!" she said, and a fresh wave of embarrassment swamped her.

"We're not teenagers. We can do whatever we want."

"Your dad was about to pull a shotgun on you."

Jack rolled his eyes.

"I'm sorry, I panicked." Callie slipped into some panties, pulled a sundress over her head. Saw Jack's eyes flare with interest at her braless state. How could he even think about sex at a time like this? Then she remembered she'd just been noticing his lack of shorts.

She ran a brush through her hair.

"Goodness knows what this will do to their fragile state," he said. "What are we going to tell them?"

"The truth." She wished she had time to brush her teeth, but it would give her an unfair advantage over Jack, and their two minutes were almost up. "That we got married and now we're getting a divorce. It'll seem very simple alongside what they're going through. How do I look?"

"Almost as good as you do naked," he said gruffly.

Callie blushed, which shouldn't be possible after what they'd done last night. Must be the presence of Brenda and Dan in the living room. With shaky hands, she ran a lipstick over her lips, but made such a mess she had to wipe it off with a tissue.

"I'll do the talking," Jack said.

She was coward enough to agree.

DAN WAS PACING the living room. Callie could tell from the way his eyes moved that he was automatically checking the quality of Jack's paint job. That, at least, would withstand scrutiny.

"Well," Dan demanded, as if they were indeed teenagers. "What the heck is going on?"

Callie opened her mouth, but a glare from Jack made her close it again.

"If you're married," Brenda said, bewildered, "why weren't we invited to the wedding? Why aren't you wearing rings?"

"Mom, Dad." Jack put an arm around Callie. "You're not going to like what I'm about to tell you, but please hear me out."

Dan growled, "There'd better be a good explanation."

"It's *an* explanation," Jack said flatly. "Callie and I got married eight years ago."

Brenda screeched. Dan's brows lowered. Like father, like son, Callie thought.

"Callie's mom knew about it," Jack said hurriedly, seeing his father doing the math. "It was all legal. You remember how upset Jenny was about the custody claim from Callie's grandparents."

"She was terrified of those people," Brenda admitted.

"But why did you have to get married?" Dan asked. "You could have talked to us. We could have worked something out."

Jack swallowed, and Callie knew he wasn't looking forward to admitting his true motives. But they'd agreed they would tell the truth.

"This was right after Lucy's death," he said. "I was about to move to England. You guys were so cut up about Lucy, and I needed—*wanted*—to get to Oxford, so I—"

Callie couldn't let him lower himself in his parents' estimation. "Jack was worried that you two would suffer even more hurt if I left," she said. "I was the strongest link you had with Lucy, and he didn't want you to lose that."

Jack glanced at her. "But also—"

"Also," Callie said, "Mom was worried about my financial security, and Jack promised he would see that I was okay. That promise meant a lot to my mom."

It was all true.

Jack opened his mouth again. Good grief, what was with this urge to confess? Callie glared at him until he closed it.

"Jack did me and my mom a favor," she said.

Dan looked downright skeptical, and Brenda frowned as if she was still trying to find the missing link.

"The marriage was in name only," Callie stated quickly. Then she blushed.

"That's not what it looked like in there." Dan jerked his thumb toward the bedroom.

Jack moved half in front of her, as if to shield her. "That was a recent development," he said. "Very recent."

"Callie's like a daughter to us," Dan said. "You'd better not be playing with her feelings."

"We're adults," Jack replied. "What we do is our business."

Dan seemed about to disagree strongly, but Brenda touched her husband's hand. Hesitantly at first, then she gripped his fingers.

"Dan...darling," she said.

They were back to *darling?* Callie saw Dan's hand twitch in Brenda's. Then he squared his shoulders as if he would accept her touch, her endearments, accept *her,* even if it killed him. When Brenda and Dan had got married, they'd known it was forever.

"Getting married the way these two did was dumb, especially for Jack. Callie was too young to know better," Brenda said. "But think of it this way—everything has turned out just right."

The situation was so far from right, for all of them, that Callie almost laughed.

"Uh, what do you mean?" Jack asked.

Brenda spread her hands. "We've been worried about you for years, Jack, whether you'd ever get time to find a nice girl. And now you've found the nicest girl of all. One we already love as a daughter." She opened her arms to Callie. "Sweetie, you really are our daughter now."

When Callie didn't move, Jack's mother came forward and enveloped her in a hug that she automatically returned. "Brenda, there's something…"

Over the woman's shoulder she sent Jack a pleading, urgent appeal that said, *Set the record straight. Now.*

Dan clapped his son on the back. "I guess your mom's right." Then he hugged Jack. "You couldn't have made a better choice. I'm proud of your good sense." He turned to Callie. "Brenda and I actually came by for that breakfast you offered us. Thought we'd better make an effort to patch things up all around. But how about we go out for breakfast, to celebrate?"

Jack caught another desperate look from Callie. This was where he needed to say, *Actually, Dad, Mom, we're getting a divorce.*

He couldn't do it. As he accepted a hug from his mom, he transmitted a silent apology to Callie. "Dad, maybe we should keep this more low-key. Callie and I would appreciate if you wouldn't tell anyone we're married just yet," Jack said.

"Why not?"

"We haven't been, uh, close—" Callie blushed adorably, Jack thought "—very long, and it's too soon to say if it's going to last."

"Of course it'll last," Dan said. "Mitchell marriages always do." He cocked his head toward Brenda, who nodded.

"Dad, we're still getting used to the idea," Jack said firmly. "We haven't talked about the future—"

"Where you'll live," Brenda interjected. She gasped. "Jack, you're leaving town next week! Are you taking Callie away?"

He said a silent, sad goodbye to his plans to get back to work, and made the ultimate sacrifice. "I've decided to stay another couple of weeks—" Callie's eyes widened "—so we have time to figure things out." *To get up the guts to tell you we're divorcing.* "This attraction is pretty sudden. We don't even know if we're compatible."

"You shouldn't be up to hanky-panky if you're not compatible," Dan said.

Callie cried off on breakfast with the excuse that she didn't have time before the shop opened. At last, Jack's parents left.

Jack watched them as they walked down the front path. At least they were talking to each other, even if it was without much enthusiasm.

He closed the door and leaned on it. What the hell had he done? He'd let his libido get the better of his good sense, and instead of him being well on the way to his divorce, his parents were picturing him and Callie living happily ever after.

Then he remembered the amazing night they'd just shared, the feel of her beautiful body beneath his, knowing Callie more intimately than he'd known anyone else, and it was hard not to feel it was worth it.

"That was the worst moment of my life," Callie exclaimed.

Jack caught her in his arms and kissed her thoroughly.

After a minute, she thumped his chest. "You can't fix it with a kiss. This stops right now. No more 'hanky-panky.'"

He sighed and let her go. "You're right."

Callie was pretty sure the hunger in Jack's eyes was reflected in her own. She hadn't showered, she hadn't put on moisturizer and she felt gritty. The skin on her face was taut. But she wanted Jack and he wanted her.

She felt quite heroic as she walked away from him.

"There's another possibility." He followed her to the kitchen. "An alternative to 'no more hanky-panky.'"

She caught her breath. "What's that?"

"Seeing as we're already married, and getting out of the marriage is becoming more complicated by the minute…" He hesitated.

"Yes?" She had a sudden inkling what was coming next.

"If we think there's any chance of what we have—" he waved a hand to encompass them both "—turning into a serious relationship, now's the time to make that call."

Was he suggesting he might want that? Callie's heart beat faster; she stole a glance at him. Nothing showed in his face. She could imagine him looking like this—calm and neutral—when he had to deliver bad news to patients.

He hadn't even said he liked her, let alone loved her.

She needed coffee she decided, and began to fill the kettle. Over her shoulder, she said, "You're still planning to go back to England, right? And then maybe France?"

He nodded. "Is that a show-stopper? Are you saying you'd never consider moving with your husband?" He leaned against the island. "I guess the cottage and your shop would have to be a consideration."

She'd never thought about it, but she knew the answer. "As your friend Adam said, it's who you're with, not where you are that matters." She put the kettle on the stove. "I'd give up anything, go anywhere for a husband I loved and who loved me."

Jack didn't declare his love for her.

"Why would you even consider staying married to me?" she asked.

He walked over to the kitchen window to stare outside. "You're bright and smart, hardworking." He sounded as if he was considering hiring her. "I'm fond of you," he said, "and you're good company." He turned back to face her. "I love making love with you."

"You're still thinking your parents will move with you?"

"Yes," he said defensively. "Eventually. If you're with me, that would be an even greater incentive for them. But in the meantime we could come back to Parkvale more regularly than I have." He took the French press down from its shelf and handed it to her. "Maybe Mom and Dad would move when we started a family. I'd like to have kids, and you would, too."

That was rather a drastic way to make his parents happy.

"Those things you said to me the other day," she began. "About my desire to have a family and how completely I've failed."

"I was too harsh. I'm sorry."

She shook her head. "You were right. Jack, I can't go into a marriage—a family—where it's not about me. I can't stay on the sidelines."

"You wouldn't be on the sidelines," he said. "Mom and Dad are going to love you even more."

He realized the implication of what he'd said, of what he hadn't said, and he colored.

"I'd be on *your* sidelines." Callie verbalized it for him. "I'd be supporting your career, raising your kids, helping with your parents."

She saw from his flash of guilt that he recognized the truth in what she said.

"You've changed over the past few weeks, in a good way," she continued. "But although you've helped me and you've stepped up to the plate for your parents, you're only doing it to set everything in order so you can leave. So that your life can go on the way you planned." She realized this wasn't going to turn into a cozy cup of coffee, and took the kettle off the stove. "Jack, I want a man whose life is about me, just as my life would be about him."

Slowly, regretfully, he nodded. "So we're agreed. We go ahead with the divorce."

She'd known that was the only outcome, but still it hurt to know he could never want her that much.

Callie nodded in turn. "Let's give your parents a couple of weeks to get their lives back on track, and to see we're really not suited to each other. Then we'll tell them."

CHAPTER SIXTEEN

JACK WASN'T SURPRISED by the disappointment he felt when Callie turned down his suggestion that they stay married. He was fond of her, and it had been the perfect solution to a lot of things. But he understood her reasons for rejecting him. If he'd been an impartial observer, he'd have suggested she tell him to get lost.

What surprised him was that by Sunday, a week later, he was still just as disappointed.

Irritated over anything and everything, he didn't exactly endear himself to Callie as he tiled the floor in her second bathroom. He'd already snapped at her twice today, and she was now handing him tile spacers in stony silence. His bad mood hadn't had a positive effect on his parents, either. Brenda's and Dan's attempts at reconciliation were halting, at best. They were talking to each other, very politely, but there was none of the spontaneous affection between them that Jack had always taken for granted.

He wasn't sure which of them he wanted to shake most. His mom, for insisting she and Dan had to talk through every detail of Lucy's life and death before they could heal the rift, or his dad, for bringing up the demolition of the memorial bench at every opportunity.

The only good thing, he told himself, was that his parents had shut up about his and Callie's marriage. He suspected they knew in their hearts it wasn't going to work out.

But his marriage had never been designed to work out. His parents' had.

If only he knew what to say to them that would make a difference. It would be so much easier if their problem was something to do with physical health. As Callie said, he often ascribed physical causes to emotional reactions...but, heck, that's what he was best at.

Jack sat back on his heels. "It's time I talked some sense into Mom and Dad."

"Not exactly your strong point to date," Callie said acidly.

"Let's go." He got to his feet. "Come with me and you can kick me hard if I say the wrong thing."

"That might be fun," she conceded.

THE AFTERNOON WAS DRIZZLY, so Dan wasn't working outside, as he normally would on a Sunday. They found Brenda kneading dough in the kitchen, and Dan checking hardware supplier invoices in the den.

Jack shepherded them both into the dining room, where they all sat around the table.

"I want to talk about fixing up whatever's wrong between you two," he said.

Neither of his parents looked thrilled to be discussing their marriage with him.

"Just listen to what Jack has to say," Callie begged.

"It might help." She didn't sound that convinced, but Brenda murmured her agreement, and Dan gave a sharp nod of his head.

"From where I'm sitting," Jack said bluntly, "you guys aren't making much progress."

Callie closed her eyes.

"That's because you're coming at this the wrong way," he said. "Mom, you're hung up on what Dad did or didn't feel or say about Lucy's death. Dad, you're more worried about Mom eroding your comfort zone than you are about your own feelings or hers."

His father's jaw set tight.

"Those things are just symptoms," Jack said. "Treating the symptoms is only meant for temporary alleviation of pain. It doesn't treat the cause."

Under the table, Callie kicked him hard.

Jack laughed. "Have a little faith in me, sweetheart." The "sweetheart" slipped out; he hoped no one had noticed. "Or at least have faith in your ability to make me see sense. For once, I'm not about to turn this into a medical issue."

He pushed his chair back and stood. He paced to the far end of the room. "Maybe it is kind of medical—" he ignored the twitch of Callie's foot that suggested he was due another kick "—because this is about the heart. Your broken hearts."

"What are you talking about?" Dan barked.

"That's my diagnosis," Jack said. "You're both suffering from untreated heartbreak over Lucy's death. Because you each have a different way of handling grief, you both tried to cope in your own way, alone. Which was a big mistake."

"I couldn't do it your father's way," Brenda said. "I can't bottle up my feelings."

"You guys are best when you do things together. You always have been." Jack strode back to the table and planted his hands on his chair. "This is the one time you tried to do things separately, and you made a total mess of it."

"Tactful," Callie muttered.

"We're way past the need for tact here," he said. "Mom, Dad, I shouldn't have rushed away so soon after Lucy's death, and I'm sorry. You needed everyone you loved around you, and I wasn't here. If I had been, maybe you guys would have pulled together better, the way you always did when we were kids." He chuckled. "Lucy and I always knew that when you two united on something, we'd never get our own way."

Brenda made a sound that was half laugh, half sob.

Dan rubbed a fist over his chest. "What do you suggest we do about this supposed heartbreak?"

"From now on, you're in this together," Jack said. "If Dad wants to build another bench, Mom, you'll be right there beside him hammering nails. Dad, if Mom wants to firebomb the school to protest about Lucy's Lifesavers, you're going to light the match."

Callie's eyes widened.

"I didn't mean that about firebombing, Mom," he said.

"I know you didn't, sweetie," she replied.

"The main thing is, what's important to you when it comes to remembering Lucy, Dad, should be just as important to Mom. And vice versa. And I want you both in counseling. Together."

"I don't—" Dan began, but Brenda grabbed his wrist and pressed a kiss to his palm. "Fine." He held on to her hand.

"It's fine with me, too," Brenda said. "Dan, if you'll let me help, we'll build the most beautiful bench ever for Lucy. I love you so much. No one else could ever be as good for me as you are." She stood and kissed him.

The kiss lasted long enough that Jack glanced at his watch. When his parents surfaced, Dan had his arms wrapped awkwardly around his wife.

"You're a piece of work, Brenda." He squeezed her tightly. "My life's work."

JACK LEFT HIS PARENTS canoodling in the dining room, and drove Callie back to her cottage.

"I'll finish those tiles in the next couple of days," he said.

"Great." She unclipped her seat belt. "You did a good thing back there, Jack."

"Yeah, not bad." He was grinning. Somehow her modest praise meant more to him than the accolades of a hundred peers or patients.

She got out of the car before he could claim the kiss that might have been the expected reward for a guy who'd just patched up his parents' marriage. Ah, well, there was always tomorrow.

Though not many more tomorrows with Callie, he realized.

As he neared his parents' home, again his cell phone rang, a number he didn't recognize. He pulled over to take the call.

It was the private detective he'd hired to find Callie's grandparents.

"I found them," Mark Haines said.

Jack buzzed his window down, rested his elbow on the sill. "They're still in Monterey? Did you talk to them?"

"They're in Monterey, but they're not talking to anyone."

"I heard they were stubborn...." Jack's image of a tender reunion between Callie and her grandparents began to slowly dissolve.

"William Summers is eighty-two. He had a stroke a few years back and has been in long-term care since. He has virtually no movement, though the doctors think his brain is ticking along okay."

"Poor guy," Jack said. He heard a beep on his phone, another call coming in; he ignored it. "What about the grandmother?"

He heard the rustle of flipping pages over the line.

"Mona Summers, also eighty-two, is in care, with advanced Alzheimer's disease. She hasn't recognized anyone in some time."

Jack sagged back against the headrest. "Short of them both being dead, things couldn't be worse."

"I checked out their circumstances," Haines said. "As far as I can tell, they have no other relatives. I don't know how they've left their estate, which appears substantial even after the medical bills they've incurred. But Ms. Summers would have a legitimate claim to an inheritance."

"That won't matter to Callie," Jack said. Though

it might help *him* sleep at night, knowing she was more secure.

"I tried to discover more about Ms. Summers's father and his relationship with his parents," Haines said. "I spoke to neighbors—not always the best indicator, mind you—as well as friends, colleagues, church members. And some former friends."

Once again, the beep of another call distracted Jack. "What did you conclude?" he asked.

Haines hemmed and hawed. "William and Mona Summers had just the one child, Stephen—your wife's father. The boy got onto drugs in his teens. By all accounts he was a waste of space. His parents decided to practice tough love—had him kidnapped and taken into rehab."

"It didn't work," Jack guessed.

"The kid ran away, so his parents cut him off, still sticking with tough love, hoping that when he ran out of money he'd clean up his act. He did, for a while at least, but he didn't go back home. Apparently he died about three years ago."

A beep indicated another call coming through; whoever it was was persistent. Jack shut out the distraction. "Any idea why they turned Callie down when she tried to resume contact a few years ago?"

"That I couldn't find out," the investigator said.

Jack wrapped up the call soon after. Why was it that as soon as he got one family fire under control, another one blew up?

Not only was Callie never going to have the love of her grandparents, but now Jack had to break the news of their condition to her. She would want to visit them, and she would add them to her list of people to worry about.

Which meant he would worry about her more.

Jack cursed. He turned the car around and headed back for Callie's house. He had about five minutes to decide how he was going to play this.

The most obvious problem was that Callie wanted—*needed*—a family of her own. And Jack's last chance of giving her one had crashed and burned.

I could be her family. He glanced in the rearview mirror, beset by the feeling he was being chased. No one there—what did he expect on a Sunday afternoon in Parkvale?

He reminded himself he'd already suggested to Callie that they should stick together, and she'd sensibly refused. She knew the truth: Jack wasn't interested in the kind of family life she wanted.

Life with Callie would be one long chain of family obligations. And she wouldn't accept any excuses for him skipping them, even if he was the number one neurosurgeon on the planet.

She'd want a full-time dad for her kids, a loving, dedicated husband.

Maybe he should encourage her to get together with Rob. The guy was nuts about her. He'd do everything to make Callie happy.

Jack realized he'd clenched his fingers around the steering wheel so tightly his knuckles were white. He eased off.

Yeah, she could marry Rob, and Jack wouldn't think about the details. She'd share Rob's bed, have Rob's kids... Okay, this was stupid. Somehow he'd let the car get up to fifty miles per hour in a thirty-mile area. He slowed down.

She didn't want Rob. If she did, she could have had him by now. Did she want Jack, despite what she'd said? Did he really want her?

The thoughts chased in circles around his head.

He'd done what he could for Callie, but now it didn't feel like enough. Something tugged at his heart, trying to yank his innermost feelings out of him and put them on display.

He didn't want those kinds of feelings—the kind that made a guy forget the life he had mapped out.

Damn, he would miss Callie when he went back to England.

I'll get a girlfriend. But would he find one who'd tell him when he was getting too big for his boots?

Okay, maybe Callie could be his girlfriend. They could date without a long-term commitment, after the divorce came through. She could visit him in England; they could go to France.

It wouldn't kill him to lighten up in his attitude to his work, take a vacation. Of course, she wouldn't vacation with him if she was married to Rob.

Maybe he should just propose to Callie, and tell her he would do his best to put her first in his life. Alternatively, maybe he should inform her he was leaving town soon, and if she wanted a good guy, she should go after Rob.

She was reversing out of her driveway when Jack pulled up outside the cottage. When she saw him, she got out of the car and ran to him.

The sight of her lifted Jack's heart…until he saw her face.

"I was coming to find you," she said breathlessly. "Your cell was busy."

"Is it Mom?" he asked, catching her anxiety.

"Your colleague, Jeremy. He's been trying your cell, then he called your mom and she gave him my number."

Jack glanced at his watch. It was late night in Oxford; Jeremy must still be pulling night shifts.

Jack got out of the car and hit the speed dial.

"Hey." He realized he'd slipped back into the American-style greeting. "Hi," he amended. "You called?"

"Jack." Jeremy sounded distracted.

"Is this a bad time?" If there was a full-blown emergency, his associate would have consulted someone else by now, and Jack should let him get on with the job.

"Jack," Jeremy said again. And Jack recognized the compassion in his voice.

He went cold. "No," he said sharply. He'd heard that sharpness before from parents, friends, grandparents who didn't want to hear.

Callie took a hesitant step toward him, obviously guessing what was coming.

"Hannah died this afternoon." Jeremy's voice was soft but clear. "She had a sudden, massive bleed."

No! "Did you excise the AVM?" Jack demanded.

"It was too deep in the brain."

"Did it show up on the angio?"

"Of course. The only way we could get at it was through radiosurgery. But you know that's not an instant fix. Jack, we ran out of time."

Ugly pain twisted inside Jack. "Her parents…"

"They're devastated," Jeremy said.

They'd been relying on Jack to heal their daughter. Callie clasped Jack's free hand in both hers, her face pale with concern. He turned away, but didn't pull out of her grip.

"Tell me exactly what happened, start to finish," he ordered.

Jack interjected a couple of questions, but from the way Jeremy told it, there was indeed nothing the team could have done. Just one of those freakish medical outcomes that serve to remind doctors they are not God.

But maybe, if I'd been there… He ended the call, stood staring at his phone for a long time as the possibilities chased through his mind.

"Jack?" Callie said. "It's Hannah, isn't it?"

Her face went hazy in front of him. He blinked, then blinked again. That was better. "She died this afternoon."

"I'm so sorry." Callie wrapped her arms around him, and for a moment he yielded to her softness, to the welcome of her embrace.

When he'd found a measure of comfort, he pulled away. "I should have been there."

She pursed her lips and said carefully, "How much difference would that have made?"

"I might have seen something, thought of something…." Harshly, he said, "If I hadn't been stuck here playing Happy Families, Hannah might have lived."

She flinched. "You're a great doctor, but you're not perfect," she said. "Maybe you're overestimating your importance."

Callie's words had come out wrong. She'd wanted to let Jack know that he couldn't shoulder all the responsibility for what had to be a team effort. "I'm sorry, I didn't mean it like that."

He gazed into the distance.

She grabbed his arm. "Jack, you don't have to bear this on your own."

"I can handle it," he said grimly. "She's not the last patient I'll lose."

"You can't switch it off, remember?" she said. "You'll never be able to stop thinking, *what if.* Jack, every minute of every day is a what-if, and we'll never know those answers. That's why you have your family—" she swallowed "—and you have me. We're here to see you through those times when the question gets too painful."

For a long moment he looked at her. Then he said, "Callie, Hannah's death isn't the only bad news today. I need to tell you about your grandparents."

By the time he finished, her mind was reeling. Jack had hired someone to find her grandparents…. They were ill, both beyond communication with her…and her father was dead.

Callie leaned against the rickety picket fence. "I need to go and see them."

"I figured you would." Jack touched her shoulder. "I'm sorry, Callie."

She lifted her chin. "It's not as if I've lost something I had. Just an opportunity that never really existed." She saw in his eyes that his apology was about more than her ill grandparents. "You're leaving." She grabbed hold of the fence to counter her sudden light-headedness.

Jack nodded. "I'm going back to England."

CHAPTER SEVENTEEN

AS CALLIE EXPECTED, once Jack made up his mind, he completed the preparations for his departure with ruthless efficiency. He finished painting the outside of the cottage in two days flat, and made sure his parents had a counseling appointment. He even bought a wedding present for his cousin Sarah and delivered it to Aunt Nancy's house.

Brenda and Dan apparently understood his need to return to Oxford, and tactfully refrained from asking Callie about the status of her marriage. Callie supposed that in the weeks to come, they would realize it was over, and by the time she and Jack finally announced the fact, no one would be surprised. Or hurt.

Except her.

Get used to it, she told herself on the day of his departure as she poured a bowl of cornflakes. She would have to get used to Jack not being here when she needed him. She'd never realized it, but she needed him every bit as much as Brenda and Dan did. From now on she would have to have dinner with his parents, arrange flowers, renovate houses, live her life…breathe…without Jack.

In the month that he'd been home, so much had

changed. Brenda and Dan had begun the process of healing. Jack had become a different man from the arrogant surgeon who'd showed up in her shop that first day. The cottage was transformed.

The only thing that hadn't changed, Callie realized, was her. She choked on her cereal, thumped her chest to make sure no stray cornflakes were trapped in her lungs.

Could it be true that after all that had happened in the past few weeks, she hadn't changed?

"I fell in love with Jack," she told the cartoon clown on the milk carton in front of her. "That was different."

Okay, so she'd fallen in love with him. And now she was letting the one man she wanted to be with for the rest of her life walk away.

Jack would say she was doing what she always did. Deciding, unconsciously, not to fight for the family she wanted.

"It wasn't my decision," she protested. "He doesn't love me, and I can't settle for less."

The milk carton clown grinned back at her.

I didn't ask for more. Sure, she'd told Jack what she wanted in a man. But she'd never told him *he* was the man she wanted. She'd challenged him to love his parents, but let him off the hook when it came to loving her.

Callie pushed her half-finished cereal away. She'd spent weeks fighting Jack for his parents' sake. Now she was going to fight him for hers.

The clock on the oven read 7:00 a.m. Any minute now, Jack would be leaving for Memphis to catch his afternoon flight.

SHE'D BEEN ON THE ROAD two or three minutes when she saw a black Jaguar coming toward her. Fast.

The good news was, this wasn't the road out of town. Callie laughed out loud as she realized that fighting for her man wasn't going to be an all-out, bloody battle. She flashed her headlights at Jack. He sped past her before he recognized the Honda. Then Callie heard the squeal of brakes.

Jack reversed up the road until his window was even with hers. He looked a lot more together than she did—she hadn't even combed her hair.

"Your place," he said. "Now."

He drove off without waiting for her agreement.

Good grief, was this what life with him would be like? Callie sighed and turned around, following him home at a very sedate pace. She could at least make him wait.

He was inside her kitchen—she'd forgotten to lock the door—holding an enormous bouquet of flowers. "What took you so long?" he said. "And what happened to your hair?" He looked more closely. "Your T-shirt is inside-out."

"I was in a hurry." Callie recognized the Darling Buds sticker attached to the flowers. She looked at the blooms...and started to laugh. Hot pink gerberas, interspersed with green and yellow Zantedeschia.

"I know," he said, "it's horrible. But you said they're your favorites."

Who sends flowers to a florist?

Jack does.

Her heart swelled. "I never meant them to go together," she said, still laughing. She took the flowers from him, buried her nose in the ugliest, most beautiful bouquet she'd ever seen.

"I never meant you and me to go together," Jack said morosely. "It just goes to show."

Callie dropped the flowers on the island and wrapped her arms around his neck. Automatically, his hands went to her bottom.

"You can't forgive me this easily," he protested. "I've been a jerk."

She sighed. "I daresay it won't be the last time."

He laughed, then bent to kiss her.

Callie clapped a hand over her mouth. "I need to brush my teeth," she said in a muffled voice.

"I daresay it won't be the last time I kiss you before you brush your teeth."

She couldn't argue with his logic.

When he resurfaced, he said, half teasing, half serious, "One of us is going to have to say it first. One of us has to admit that we can't live without the other."

Her happiness bloomed like spring flowers, and Callie could hardly breathe. "I think it should be you."

"You're right, as always." He dropped a kiss on her nose. "I love you, Callie. I need you to be my wife, for real and for always."

"You're not just, what was it, fond of me?"

He swatted her behind. "I'm crazy in love with you and there's no damn way out of it. I packed my bag and realized there was no way I could get on that plane without you. We're staying married, or remarrying, or whatever we need to do to be together forever."

She pressed against him, felt his response. "Okay."

Jack's smile grew impossibly tender. "I want you to share the load with me, the way you said. I want to share your life, your worries, from your grandparents to your rats."

He kissed her boldly, thoroughly, until she shook with need.

"You haven't told me you love me," he murmured against her ear. "Am I assuming too much?" She reveled in the hint of insecurity in his voice.

"You know you already have far too big an opinion of yourself." Her voice trembled, from a crazy desire to laugh and cry. "I can't imagine how impossible you'll be if I tell you how much I love you."

He pulled away, grasped her hands. "I'm afraid I must insist."

She sighed. "Okay, but could I just say that I can change my mind at any time?"

"Over my dead body," he growled.

"I love you, Jack, for always, with every breath in my body. I love you for your kindness to your family and to your patients, for your commitment to doing your very best. For the way you admit you're wrong—"

"I never do that," he said, outraged.

She slapped his arm. "You just did, by coming here today. I love the way you saw the truth about me where no one else did." She leaned forward, kissed his mouth.

"Anything else?" he said hopefully.

"I love that you're great with a paintbrush." She giggled as he began to tickle her. "Okay, okay, I love that you're good in bed."

He tickled her harder.

"Fantastic—" she managed the word between laughing gasps "—in bed."

"That makes two of us," he said. "I can't wait to get you there again."

She wrapped her arms around his neck, pulled him down to her for a heated kiss that held the promise of a lifetime.

"I'd better tell you my plan for us," Jack said at last. "So that you can pull it to shreds and tell me I'm wrong."

"If this kissing is part of it, so far I'm liking it a lot."

"You need to get out of Parkvale, for a while at least," he said. "And I need some time alone with you. I've talked to my boss and agreed that we'll spend a year in Paris. Then I'll try to organize a one-year consulting residency somewhere like New York, where I can renew my local contacts. If that works for you."

"It sounds wonderful." Callie tried to get her head around the fact that she might be about to spend an extended period in two of the world's greatest cities. "What happens after that?"

He kissed her. "Then we move back to Memphis, and I start work at Northcross Hospital."

"But you said there's no center of neurosurgical excellence there," she said, dismayed that he would even consider moving out of his specialty. "Jack, you can't give up neurosurgery. I'll live wherever you need to be."

He kissed her hard. "I appreciate the offer, sweetheart, but it's more accurate to say there's no center of neurosurgical excellence there *yet*. There will be by the time I've established one. In fact," he said smugly,

"I wouldn't be surprised if it's the best in the U.S.A. in ten years' time."

"You are so arrogant," she said admiringly.

He inclined his head. "Luckily, I've got you to stop me from getting too big for my stethoscope."

She tutted. "It'll be a full-time job."

"Do you think you can fit in raising a couple of kids?"

"Absolutely." She beamed.

Jack kissed her until they both ran out of breath.

"We'll keep your cottage," he said, "and come for weekends—bring the kids to see their grandparents. I'm thinking maybe after we've been doing that for five years, Dad will trust me enough to discuss his blood pressure."

She laughed, and then she was too busy kissing him to say more. His hands roamed her, found the curves he craved. She sighed with longing, then pulled back.

"Doctor, Doctor," she said, and he was smiling already. "I'm in love with my husband."

Jack caught her up in another kiss, one that melted her insides.

"Incurable," he diagnosed with supreme satisfaction.

* * * * *

'I'VE FOUND HER.'

Max froze.

It was what he'd been waiting for since June, but now—now he was almost afraid to voice the question. His heart stalling, he leaned slowly back in his chair and scoured the investigator's face for clues. 'Where?' he asked, and his voice sounded rough and unused, like a rusty hinge.

'In Suffolk. She's living in a cottage.'

Living. His heart crashed back to life, and he sucked in a long, slow breath. All these months he'd feared—

'Is she well?'

'Yes, she's well.'

He had to force himself to ask the next question. 'Alone?'

The man paused. 'No. The cottage belongs to a man called John Blake. He's working away at the moment, but he comes and goes.'

God. He felt sick. So sick he hardly registered the next few words, but then gradually they sank in. 'She's got *what?*'

'Babies. Twin girls. They're eight months old.'

'Eight—?' he echoed under his breath. 'They must be his.'

He was thinking out loud, but the P.I. heard and corrected him.

'Apparently not. I gather they're hers. She's been there since mid-January last year, and they were born during the summer—June, the woman in the post office thought. She was more than helpful. I think there's been a certain amount of speculation about their relationship.'

He'd just bet there had. God, he was going to kill her. Or Blake. Maybe both of them.

'Of course, looking at the dates, she was presumably pregnant when she left you, so they could be yours, or she could have been having an affair with this Blake character before…'

He glared at the unfortunate P.I. 'Just stick to your job. I can do the math,' he snapped, swallowing the unpalatable possibility that she'd been unfaithful to him before she'd left. 'Where is she? I want the address.'

'It's all in here,' the man said, sliding a large envelope across the desk to him. 'With my invoice.'

'I'll get it seen to. Thank you.'

'If there's anything else you need, Mr Gallagher, any further information—'

'I'll be in touch.'

'The woman in the post office told me Blake was away at the moment, if that helps,' he added quietly, and opened the door.

Max stared down at the envelope, hardly daring to open it, but when the door clicked softly shut behind the P.I., he eased up the flap, tipped it and felt his breath jam in his throat as the photos spilled out over the desk.

Oh, lord, she looked gorgeous. Different, though. It took him a moment to recognise her, because she'd grown her hair, and it was tied back in a ponytail, making her look younger and somehow freer. The blond highlights were gone, and it was back to its natural soft golden-brown, with a little curl in the end of the ponytail that he wanted to thread his finger through and tug, just gently, to draw her back to him.

Crazy. She'd put on a little weight, but it suited her. She looked well and happy and beautiful, but oddly, considering how desperate he'd been for news of her for the past year—one year, three weeks and two days, to be exact—it wasn't only Julia who held his attention after the initial shock. It was the babies sitting side by side in a supermarket trolley. Two identical and absolutely beautiful little girls.

* * * * *

When Max Gallagher hires a P.I. to find his estranged wife, Julia, he discovers she's not alone—she has twin baby girls, and they might be his. Now workaholic Max has just two weeks to prove that he can be a wonderful husband and father to the family he wants to treasure.

Look for
TWO LITTLE MIRACLES
by Caroline Anderson,
available February 2009
from Harlequin Romance®

HARLEQUIN® Romance®

This February the Harlequin® Romance series
will feature six Diamond Brides stories featuring
diamond proposals and gorgeous grooms.

Share your dream wedding proposal and you could WIN!

The most romantic entry will win a diamond
necklace and will inspire a proposal in one of
our upcoming Diamond Grooms books in 2010.

In 100 words or less, tell us the most romantic
way that you dream of being proposed to.

For more information, and to enter
the Diamond Brides Proposal contest, please visit
www.DiamondBridesProposal.com

Or mail your entry to us at:

IN THE U.S.: 3010 Walden Ave., P.O. Box 9069, Buffalo, NY 14269-9069
IN CANADA: 225 Duncan Mill Road, Don Mills, ON M3B 3K9

REQUEST YOUR FREE BOOKS!
2 FREE NOVELS PLUS 2 FREE GIFTS!

HARLEQUIN®

Super Romance®

Exciting, emotional, unexpected!

YES! Please send me 2 FREE Harlequin Superromance® novels and my 2 FREE gifts (gifts are worth about $10). After receiving them, if I don't wish to receive any more books, I can return the shipping statement marked "cancel." If I don't cancel, I will receive 6 brand-new novels every month and be billed just $4.69 per book in the U.S. or $5.24 per book in Canada, plus 25¢ shipping and handling per book and applicable taxes, if any*. That's a savings of close to 15% off the cover price! I understand that accepting the 2 free books and gifts places me under no obligation to buy anything. I can always return a shipment and cancel at any time. Even if I never buy another book from Harlequin, the two free books and gifts are mine to keep forever.

135 HDN EEX7   336 HDN EEYK

Name	(PLEASE PRINT)	
Address		Apt. #
City	State/Prov.	Zip/Postal Code

Signature (if under 18, a parent or guardian must sign)

Mail to the **Harlequin Reader Service:**
IN U.S.A.: P.O. Box 1867, Buffalo, NY 14240-1867
IN CANADA: P.O. Box 609, Fort Erie, Ontario L2A 5X3

Not valid to current subscribers of Harlequin Superromance books.

Want to try two free books from another line?
Call 1-800-873-8635 or visit www.morefreebooks.com.

* Terms and prices subject to change without notice. N.Y. residents add applicable sales tax. Canadian residents will be charged applicable provincial taxes and GST. Offer not valid in Quebec. This offer is limited to one order per household. All orders subject to approval. Credit or debit balances in a customer's account(s) may be offset by any other outstanding balance owed by or to the customer. Please allow 4 to 6 weeks for delivery. Offer available while quantities last.

Your Privacy: Harlequin is committed to protecting your privacy. Our Privacy Policy is available online at www.eHarlequin.com or upon request from the Reader Service. From time to time we make our lists of customers available to reputable third parties who may have a product or service of interest to you. If you would prefer we not share your name and address, please check here. ☐

HSR08

You're invited to join our Tell Harlequin Reader Panel!

By joining our new reader panel you will:

- Receive Harlequin® books—they are FREE and yours to keep with no obligation to purchase anything!
- Participate in fun online surveys
- Exchange opinions and ideas with women just like you
- Have a say in our new book ideas and help us publish the best in women's fiction

In addition, you will have a chance to win great prizes and receive special gifts! See Web site for details. Some conditions apply. Space is limited.

To join, visit us at
www.TellHarlequin.com.